FUTURELOVE

FUTURELOVE

a science fiction triad

Introduction by
GORDON R. DICKSON

The Bobbs-Merrill Company, Inc.
Indianapolis/New York

CONTENTS

INTRODUCTION

Everybody wants to write, it seems. Few, however, actually do so; and in turn only a few of these end up getting their work published. Indeed, ever since the early storytellers first stood up before the cave fires of stone-age hunters, a dream has persisted of some method which could turn story-making from a mysterious and individual art to something anyone with determination could do.

In the heyday of the pulps, the nineteen-twenties through the nineteen-forties, a number of systems tried to do just this, mainly by reducing a story to something called "plot," and then by further breaking down this business of plot into component parts which could then be reassembled to form the basis of a story anyone could write. It was not, of course, really necessary to learn a system to do this. Anyone could reduce a plot to its components of character, situation, problem and resolution:

CHARACTER: A young man,

SITUATION: Sure that his father has been murdered by his mother and the man she afterwards married,

PROBLEM: Is determined to make the murderers admit what they have done.

SOLUTION: He hits on the mechanism of having the murderers watch a reenactment

of their crime so that, while seeing
what they have done being performed, they betray themselves.

An excellent narrative plan, at base. The only problem is
that it requires someone who is already a skillful writer to
make the emerging story both memorable and effective, as
William Shakespeare did with *Hamlet*.

The truth of the matter has always been that the genius of
story-making lies in the individual writer and in his or her special use of the material chosen, not in the material itself. The
same idea becomes two different stories when filtered through
the minds of two different writers. Within the covers of this
book are stories by three writers, all dealing with the theme of
human love. But the fact that their theme is the same only
emphasizes the diversity of creativity and invention of the
writers themselves—which is the important element.

Anne McCaffrey, who is probably well known to most
readers of this book, examines in her story a mother love that
goes beyond the physical, in a new and different sense of that
phrase; a sense, in fact, not possible until present-day medical
technology gave us the means of realizing it. The particular
gift of Anne McCaffrey is that she can infuse such an intense
human light and warmth into a hitherto-unknown, laboratory-
cold subject that it takes on the familiar, common quality of
our everyday readerly lives.

Joan Holly, who has also been writing SF successfully for
years, deals with a different kind of parent-child pattern.
Again there is a love situation emerging out of a relationship
which would have been impossible before present-day science
gave it to us as something that could happen. But here again,
through Joan Holly's creativity, we have an intense, swift-run-

ning story, like a landslide channeled between canyon walls so deep they almost shut out the light.

Jeffrey Carver goes one step beyond the interaction of ordinary human love. He plunges the reader into a small whirlpool of individual lives, carried along with the rushing current of power, plunging ever more swiftly toward the brink of a waterfall. Here, the love is not between human and human, but between human and something else—a love that in the end betrays.

The fabric of these three stories is part of the time in which they were written. As with stories written in any period, however, their threads stretch back to the very earliest patterns of storytelling. Science fiction, which started out with the conventions of nineteenth-century fantasy, has in less than a century developed techniques peculiar to itself—techniques, however, which are now being borrowed by the mainstream of fiction.

Many mainstream writers do not realize whom they have to thank for these techniques. This is not surprising, however, since even many SF writers have no idea where the roots of their special techniques lie. Besides the old tradition of fantasy out of which it developed, science fiction itself owes a particular debt of gratitude to the nineteenth-century storytellers—not only to recognized earlier writers of the genre, such as H. G. Wells and Jules Verne, but to many of the other people then writing in Western literature, who wrote either proto-science fiction or fantasy verging on science fiction, simply as variations of the short-story forms in which they were accustomed to expressing themselves.

What began to distinguish science fiction from other writing in that early time was the idea of what might be called technologized fantasy. From this came the so-called hardware science fiction of the early pulp era—a direct descendant of the tales of Wells and Verne. This was the science fiction of rockets and

robots and other futuristic machines, and in the nineteen-thir-
ties it achieved its first real development into something like
present-day science fiction in the magazine *Astounding,* under
its editor, John W. Campbell.

John Campbell took hardware science fiction and insisted
that it have something more to it than technology. What
Campbell wanted was to tie all this into what he called an
"idea story," a story that used all the trappings of what was
then science fiction to demonstrate a logical point about Man
and his present or future possibilities.

This "idea story" was really the thematic story—a story built
around a theme. Its roots in the modern era go back to Flau-
bert's *Madame Bovary.* Following World War II, science
fiction writing began to expand into this larger area of thematic story proper; developing ever more depth and breadth in
the nineteen-fifties and -sixties, to emerge in the present dec-
ade with its emphasis on "people" stories with themes growing
out of the character and motivation of human beings in a possible world.

The three stories in this book are excellent illustrations of
exactly this metamorphosis; in a very true sense, evidence of
science fiction's coming of age in twentieth-century literature.

GORDON R. DICKSON

FUTURELOVE

THE GREATEST LOVE

Anne McCaffrey

"You certainly don't live up to your name, Doctor Craft," Louise Baxter said, acidly emphasizing my name. "I trust your degree is from a legitimate medical college. Or was it the mail order variety?"

I didn't dignify the taunt with a reply. Being a young woman, I held my Cornell Medical School diploma too valuable to debase it in argument with a psychotic.

She continued in the sweetly acerbic voice that must have made her subordinates cringe, "In the fashion industry, you quickly learn how to tell the 'looker' from the 'putter.' It's very easy to classify your sort."

I refrained from saying that her sort—Cold Calculating Female posing as Concerned Mother—was just as easy for me to classify. Her motive for this interview with her daughter's obstetrician was not only specious but despicable. Her opening remark of surprise that I was a woman had set the tone of insults for the past fifteen minutes.

"I have told you the exact truth, Mrs. Baxter. The pregnancy is proceeding normally and satisfactorily. You may interpret the facts any way you see fit." I was hoping to wind up this distasteful interview quickly. "In another five months, the truth will out."

Her exclamation of disgust at my pun was no more than I'd expected. "And you have the gall to set yourself up against the best gynecologists of Harkness Pavilion?"

"It's not difficult to keep abreast of improved techniques in uterine surgery," I said calmly.

"Ha! Quack!"

I suppressed my own anger at her insult by observing that her anger brought out all the age-lines in her face despite her artful makeup.

"I checked with Harkness before I came here," she said, trying to overwhelm me with her research. "There are no new techniques which could correct a bicornuate womb!"

"So?"

"So, don't try to con me, you charlatan," and the elegant accent faltered into a flat midwestern twang. "My daughter can't carry to term. And you know it!"

"I'll remind you of that in another five months, Mrs. Baxter." I rose to indicate that the interview was at an end.

"Ach! You women's libbers are all alike! Setting yourselves up above the best men in the country on every count!"

Although I'm not an ardent feminist, such egregious remarks are likely to change my mind, particularly when thrown in without relevance and more for spite than for sense.

"I fail to see what Women's Liberation has to do with your daughter, who is so obviously anxious to fulfill woman's basic role."

The angry color now suffused Louise Baxter's well-preserved face down to the collar of her ultrasmart man-tailored pants suit. She rose majestically to her feet.

"I'll have you indicted for malpractice, you quack!" She had control of her voice again and deliberately packed all the psychotic venom she could into her threats. "I'll sue you within an inch of your life if Cecily's sanity is threatened by your callous stupidity."

At that point the door opened to admit Esther, my office nurse, in her most aggressive attitude.

"If Mrs. Baxter is quite finished, doctor," she said, stressing the title just enough to irritate the woman further, "your next patient is waiting."

"Of all the—"

"This way, Mrs. Baxter," Esther said firmly as she shepherded the angry woman toward the door.

Mrs. Baxter stalked out, slamming the street door so hard I winced, waiting for the glass to come shattering down.

"How did that virago ever produce a sweet girl like Cecily?" I mused.

"I assume that Cecily was conceived in the normal manner," said Esther.

I sat down wearily. I'd been going since four-thirty A.M. and I didn't need a distasteful interview with Baxter's sort at five P.M. "And I assume that you heard everything on the intercom?"

"For some parts, I didn't need amplification," said my faithful office nurse at her drollest. "Since this affair started, I don't dare leave the intercom hook up. Someone's got to keep your best interests at heart."

I smiled at her ruefully. "It'll be worth it—"

"You keep telling yourself—"

"—to see that girl get a baby."

"Not to mention the kudos accruing to one Doctor Allison S. Craft, O.B., G.Y.N.?"

I gave her a quelling look which she blithely ignored. "Well," I said, somewhat deflated, "there must be something more to life than babies who insist on predawn entrances."

"Have a few yourself, then," Esther suggested with a snort, then flipped my coat off the hook and gestured for me to take off the office whites. "I'm closing up and I'm turning you out, doctor."

I went.

I had a lonely restaurant supper, though Elsie, who ran the place, tried to cheer me up. Once I got home, I couldn't settle down. I wanted someone to talk to. All right, someone to gripe to. Sometimes, like now, I regretted my bachelor-girl status. Even if I had had a man in mind, I really couldn't see much family life, the kind I wanted to enjoy, until I had a large enough practice to bring in an associate. On a twenty-four-hour off-and-on schedule that such an arrangement provided, I could hardly see marriage. Not now. Especially not now.

I poured myself a drink for its medicinal value and sat on my back porch in the late spring twilight.

So—Louise Baxter would sue me if her daughter miscarried. I wondered if she'd sue me if her daughter didn't. I'd bet a thousand bucks, and my already jeopardized professional standing, that the impeccable, youthful-looking Louise Baxter was shriveling from the mere thought of being made a "grandmother." Maybe it would affect her business reputation—or crack the secret of her actual age. Could she be fighting retirement? I laughed to myself at the whimsy. Cecily Baxter Kellogg was twenty-seven, and no way was Louise Baxter in her sixties.

However, I had told Mrs. Baxter the truth, the exact truth: the pregnancy *was* well started, and the condition of the mother *was* excellent, and everything pointed to a full-term, living child.

But I hadn't told the whole truth, for Cecily Baxter Kellogg was not carrying her own child.

Another medical "impossibility" trembled on the brink of the possible. A man may have no greater love than to lay down his life for a friend, but it's a far, far greater love that causes one woman to carry another's baby: a baby with whom she has nothing, absolutely nothing, in common, except nine months of intimacy. I amended that: this baby would have a relationship, for its proxy mother was its paternal aunt.

The memory of the extraordinary beginning of this great experiment was as vivid to me as the afternoon's interview with Mrs. Baxter. And far more heart-warming.

It was almost a year ago to this day that my appointment schedule had indicated a 2:30 patient named Miss Patricia Kellogg. Esther had underscored the "Miss" with red and also the abbreviation "p.n." for prenatal. I was known to be sympathetic to unwed mothers and had performed a great many abortions—legally, too.

There was nothing abashed about Patricia Kellogg as she walked confidently into my office, carrying a briefcase.

"I'd better explain, Dr. Craft, that I am not yet pregnant. I want to be."

"Then you need a premarital examination for conception?"

"I'm not contemplating marriage."

"That . . . ah . . . used to be the usual prelude to pregnancy."

She smiled and then casually said, "Actually, I wish to have my brother's child."

"That sort of thing is frowned on by the Bible, you know," I replied with, I thought, great equanimity. "Besides presenting rather drastic genetic risks. I'd suggest you consult a psychologist, not an obstetrician."

Again that smile, tinged with mischief now. "I wish to have the child of my brother *and* his wife!"

"Ah, that hasn't been done."

She patted the briefcase. "On a human."

"Oh, I assume you've read up on those experiments with sheep and cows. They're all very well, Miss Kellogg, but obstetrically it's not the same thing. The difficulties involved . . ."

"As nearly as I can ascertain, the real difficulty involved is *doing* it."

I rose to sit on the edge of the desk. Miss Kellogg was exactly my height seated, and I needed the difference in levels. Scarcely an unattractive woman, Patricia Kellogg would be classified by men as "wholesome," "girl-next-door," rather than the sexy bird their dreams featured. She was also not at all the type to make the preposterous statements and request she had. Recently, however, I had come to appreciate that the most unlikely women would stand up and vigorously demand their civil and human rights.

Miss Kellogg was one to keep you off balance, for as she began doling out the contents of her briefcase, she explained that her sister-in-law had a bicornuate uterus. During my internship in Cornell Medical, I had encountered such a condition. The uterus develops imperfectly, with fertile ovaries but double Fallopian tubes. The victim conceives easily enough but usually aborts within six weeks. A full-term pregnancy would be a miracle. I glanced through the clinical reports from prominent New York and Michigan hospitals, bearing out Miss Kellogg's statements and detailing five separate spontaneous abortions.

"The last time, Cecily carried to three months before aborting," Pat Kellogg said. "She nearly lost her mind with grief.

"You see, she was an only child. All her girlhood she'd dreamed of having a large family. Her mother is a very successful businesswoman, and I'd say that Cecily was a mistake as far as Louise Baxter is concerned. I remember how radiantly happy Cecily and Peter, my brother, were when she started her first pregnancy six years ago. And how undaunted she was after the first miss. You've no idea how she's suffered since. I'm sorry; maybe you do, being a woman."

I nodded, but it was obvious to me, from the intensity of her expression, that she had empathized deeply with the sister-in-law's disappointments.

"To have a child has become an obsession with her."

"Why not adoption?"

"My brother was blinded in the Vietnam War."

"Yes, I see." Now that abortions were legal, there were fewer babies to be adopted, and consequently the handicapped parent was a very poor second choice.

"Children mean a lot to Peter, too. There were just two of us: our mother died at our births. Peter and I are twins, you see. But Cecily has magnified her inability all out of proportion, especially because of Peter's blindness. She feels that . . ."

"I do understand the situation," I said sympathetically as she faltered for adequate words.

"Since I got this idea," she went on more briskly, "I've been keeping very careful charts on my temperature and menstrual cycle," and she thrust sheets at me. "I've got Cecily's for the past six years. I stole them. She's always kept them up to date." She gave me an unrepentant grin. "We're just two days apart."

I smiled at that. "If matching estrous cycles were the only problem involved . . ."

"I *know* there're many, many problems, but there is so much at stake. Really, Dr. Craft, I fear for Cecily's sanity. Oh, no, I haven't breathed a word of this to Peter or Cece . . ."

"I should hope not. I'm even wondering why you're mentioning it to me."

"Chuck Henderson said you'd be interested."

No name was less expected.

"Where did you meet Dr. Henderson?" I asked, with far more calm than I felt.

"I've been following the medical journals, and I read an article he wrote on research to correct immature uteruses . . . uteri? . . . and new methods to correct certain tendencies to abort."

I'd read the same article, written with Chuck's usual meticulous care, complete with diagrams and graphic photos of uterine operations. Not the usual reading matter for a young woman.

"Well, then, why come to me?"

"Dr. Henderson said that he hadn't done any research on implantation, but he knew someone who was interested in exogenesis and who lived right in my own town. He said there was no reason for me to traipse all the way to New York to find the brave soul I needed, and he told me to ask you how the cats were doing." She looked inquiringly at me.

The name, the question, brought back memories I had been blocking for nine years: memories (I tried to convince myself again) which were the usual sophomoric enthusiasms and dreams of changing mediocre worlds into better ones with the expert flip of a miracle scalpel.

Chuck Henderson had helped me catch the cats I had used for my early attempts at exogenesis. Cats were easy to acquire in Ithaca and a lot easier to explain to an apartment superintendent than cows or sheep. I had had, I thought, good success in my early experiments, but the outcome was thwarted by some antivivisectionists who were convinced that I was using the cats for cruel, devious pranks, and the two females which I thought I had impregnated disappeared forever beyond my control. Chuck had been a real pal throughout the stages of my doomed research, all the while caustically reminding me that good old-fashioned methods of impregnation did not arouse vivisectionists.

"He said some pretty glowing things about you, Dr. Craft, and by the time he finished talking, I *knew* you were the one person who would help me."

"I'm obliged to him."

"You should be," she replied with equal dryness. "He has the highest opinion of you as a physician and as . . . as a person."

"Flattery will get you nowhere," I said evasively and turned toward the window, aware of a variety of conflicting emotions.

"Will you at least examine our medical records?" she asked softly after respecting my silence for a long moment. "I beg you to believe my sincerity when I say that I will do anything . . . painful, tedious, disagreeable . . . anything to provide my brother and sister-in-law with a child of their own flesh and blood."

She might be right, I was thinking, when she said the real difficulty was in *doing* it. Here was the magnificent opportunity I'd once yearned for, thrust at me on an afternoon as dull as my predictable future. The adventurousness, the enthusiasm of that sophomore could now be combined with the maturity and experience of the practicing physician. I'd be a fool not to try: to be content with the unwonderful.

"From the moment you stepped into this room," I said slowly to the waiting girl, "I've had no thought of questioning either your sincerity or your preseverance, Miss Kellogg."

"You'll do it?" And she began to blush suddenly and irrelevantly.

"Would you mind not boxing me into a corner quite that quickly?"

She laughed by way of apology.

"Let's say, Miss Kellogg, that I will examine the problem in the light of present-day techniques. Which have only been partially successful, mind, on animals."

She rose and stretched out her hand to me. I took it and held it briefly, hoping only to express sympathy and respect, not a binding agreement.

"I haven't said yes," I reminded her, alarmed by the look of triumph in her eyes.

"No, but I'm damned sure you will, once you've read all this." And she transferred half a dozen Department of Agriculture pamphlets and other miscellaneous printed documents from her briefcase to my desk. At the door, she turned back, looking contrite.

"I'm sorry about the shocking phraseology I used to attract your attention. I mean, about wanting my brother's child."

I had to laugh. "There's a bit of the showman in the most sedate of us. I'll call you in a few days."

"Grand! I won't call you," and with a warm smile she left.

I heard the street door close, and then Esther had whisked in, staring at me as if I'd changed sex or something. It was obvious that she'd had the intercom key up again.

"You're crazy if you do it, Allison," she said, her large brown eyes very wide.

"I quite agree with you, Esther."

"Of course, you're crazy if you don't at least *try*," she said, less vehemently, and with a breathiness of enthusiasm that surprised me in my level-headed nurse.

"I quite agree with you."

"Oh, be quiet, Allison Craft. Have you the least idea of the problems you're going to encounter, or are that Nobel Prize and the AMA citation already blinding you to reality? Women aren't cats . . . at least not gynecologically."

"Well, in a brief spontaneous thesis or two, I'd say the main problem would be . . ."

"Be practical, not medical," she snapped.

Esther was herself again. She keeps me out of debt, weasels the income tax down to the last fraction permissible, gets my bills paid on time, copes with hysterical primiparas, new fathers and doting grandparents, and she's a damned good R.N., too.

"And what are *your* visible monkey wrenches?" I asked her.

She held up her left hand and counted by the fingers. "Have you considered the moral issue if someone finds out she's giving birth to her brother's child?"

"A different hospital, in another town or state."

"Great time traveling was had by all. Or had you planned to transfer the fertilized egg right here in the cottage hospital before God and his little brother?"

"That's easy to wangle. At night. On an emergency basis. Everyone knows Cecily Kellogg keeps aborting, and keeps trying."

I couldn't let Esther see that she was making me find answers to contingencies I hadn't got around to considering yet. I was still trying to figure out how to flush the fertilized ovum from the womb. Fortunately, Esther doesn't second-guess me as much as she believes she does.

"You have flipped your ever-loving wig," she said, exhibiting an appreciation for current slang that I hadn't known she possessed, "but I'm awfully glad it's the Kelloggs."

"You know them?" I asked, mildly surprised.

"And so do you," she replied, exasperated. "I thought that's why you even considered such a sugar-mad scheme. Peter Kellogg? Professor Peter Kellogg?"

Recognition came: I certainly did know Peter Kellogg. The shock technique Patricia had employed had succeeded in keeping me from associating the name with a face or character. I had heard the campus chatter about Peter Kellogg's brilliant dissertations on English poets of the eighteenth century, and I'd enjoyed his own exquisite verse. As with another notable poet, blindness was only a physical condition, not necessarily a limitation, because Peter Kellogg refused to consider sightlessness a handicap. Although I had never met the man, he and his German shepherd, Wizard, were campus familiars. I had often seen the tall dogged figure as he strode the town streets or college paths. It now occurred to me that I had also seen his wife, Cecily, walking beside him. The picture of the tall couple I had all but decided to help, heaven helping me, was a very pleasurable one in my mind's eye, and I felt a surge of altruistic euphoria. Yes, I could appreciate why the sister was so determined that they should have a child. Surely here was a man who deserved progeny, if only a minor part of his brilliance could be passed along. A thought flitted through my head, causing me a spasm of mirth.

"Well?" demanded Esther, who hates missing a joke.

"The Catholic Church won't like it at all, at all."

"Like what?"

"Usurping the prerogatives of one of the Trinity."

"Okay, doctor, what's the first step?"

In the following weeks, I should have seen the psychologist, not Patricia Kellogg. But, as Esther became too fond of remarking, I was so happy butting my stone wall. Except I was certain I'd found the keystone. I augmented the pamphlets and treatises left me by Pat Kellogg with as much material as I could find on all the allied fields—endocrinology, hormones, uterine surgical techniques—and a very interesting study about successful exogenesis in rabbits.

I also went kitty-catching again, having exhumed the notes I'd made on my ill-fated college experiment. Coincident with the shadows of that disappointment was the mocking face of Chuck Henderson. I exorcised that ghost when I successfully transplanted the fertilized ova from a white pedigreed Angora to as nondescript a tabby as I could find. The other three attempts didn't fertilize properly, so I'll pass them without mention. As soon as I was assured the tabby's pregnancy was well advanced, I did a Caesarian and checked the fetuses. They were unarguably those of the Angora, and all five were perfectly formed.

There are, however, more than minor differences between the procreative apparatus of the feline and that of the human female, so that my experiments were merely reruns that proved exogenesis was possible in cats. The successful exogenetic births of sheep and cows in Texas were encouraging, but in the final analysis only added two more species in which this delicate interference with normal conception and pregnancy was possible. One minor physiological variation between humans and cows or sheep was very significant for my purposes: In human females the length of the oviducts before they unite to form the corpus uteri is short, leaving less time and space to catch the fertilized egg before it reaches the endometrium and undergoes impregnation there: at which point there can be no hope of transplantation.

This lack of time and space would prove one of the real barriers to success. It takes approximately twenty-four hours for the fertilized ova to drop from the ovaries through the Fallopian tubes into the suitably stimulated endometrium of the uterus. The sticky bit would be to catch one of Cecily's

fertilized ova before it could reach her uterus and put the cap-
tured ovum into the equally stimulated uterus of her sister-in-
law.

The fertile ova of cows, sheep and cats had been relatively
easy to flush out. To overcome the disadvantage in the human,
I planned to use one of the new gossamer-fine plastic films, in
the form of a fish-traplike contrivance (which nearly drove me
crazy to fashion). This would fit at the end of the Fallopian
tubes and, I hoped, would catch the fertilized ovum. By sur-
gically removing the bag, I could empty its contents into the
other womb, unscientifically cross my fingers and hope!

With the use of a new estrogen compound, it would be relatively simple to synchronize the estrous cycles of the two
women. Standard dilation and curettage on both uteri would
prepare the areas for the best possible results and allow me to
place the plastic film at the end of Cecily's tubes. The first
D&Cs could be legitimately performed without questions
asked. The second and subsequent dilations would, as Esther
had remarked, require a little more doing, since both girls
would have to be in the same room, under anesthesia, at the
same time. This meant the connivance of an amenable anesthe-
siologist as well as Esther and myself.

That's how Chuck Henderson got to sneak into the act. He
was Pat's suggestion, not mine. He already knew of the Plan,
she argued. He would be acceptable as an emergency anesthetist at those times when I had to dispense with the regular
man. (That also took finagling, but Esther managed it: she
never would tell me how.) The moment we contacted Chuck,
he was delighted: too delighted, it seemed to me; as if he'd
been waiting—breathlessly—to be asked. I was of several minds
about including him again, mostly for my own peace of mind,
but all reasonable arguments led to his active participation.

The day that Pat and I were able to approach the Kelloggs

with a plan of action will remain one of the most stirring memories of my life. I had called Pat, some two and a half weeks after her first visit to me, to say that I had researched sufficiently to approach the principals. I had already confirmed to her my willingness to try. I stressed the "try."

Pat arranged an evening meeting, and we arrived together at the Kelloggs' apartment, myself laden with a heavy briefcase containing twice as much material as Pat had given me. Pat was so nervous that I wondered if she feared that she might be unable to persuade the other two members of the cast to go through with the attempt.

I had to pass an entrance exam myself, executed by Wizard, Peter Kellogg's guide dog, an exceedingly beautiful tan and black specimen with beauty marks at the corners of his intelligent eyes. He stood at the door, sniffed the hand I judiciously extended, gave a sneeze as Pat told him I was a friend, and then retired to lie under the dining room table. I was awed by the inherent power in the apparently docile beast. I was glad I was considered a friend by that 125-pound fellow.

Peter Kellogg had risen as Pat drew me into the room, and Peter introduced me to his tall, too slender brunette wife.

We put off the important announcement with some chitchat, my appreciative congratulations on his latest verses in the *New Yorker,* our attempts to find mutual acquaintances. Finally, unable to endure further inanities, Pat blurted out:

"How would you like to be parents?"

Even the dog came alert in the sudden pulsing silence.

"Pat . . ." began Peter in gentle admonishment, but Cecily overrode him with a sharp, nearly hysterical "How?"

"Exogenesis," Pat said, expelling the word on a breath.

Peter and Cecily looked at me. I include Peter, because he never did fail to turn his lifeless eyes in the direction of the speaker, a habit most blind people never acquire but one which is very reassuring to the sighted. Peter always tried to avoid embarrassing people.

"I take it that you have arrived at some method of accomplishing exogenesis, doctor?" Peter asked.

"Dr. Craft *believes* it can be done," and Pat was careful, as I'd insisted she should be, not to present the plan as an established procedure. "There are problems," she said, in a masterpiece of understatement; "much to be discussed . . ."

"Who's the other mother?" asked Cecily, jumping a giant step ahead.

Peter turned unerringly toward his sister. At Cecily's gasping sob, Wizard gave a low whine. Peter quietly reassured him.

"I had a suspicion you'd been up to something, Pat," he said dryly. "I hardly anticipated something as momentous as this. Smacks of the incestuous, I'd say, doesn't it, doctor?"

"Peter! How can you even mention such a thing in connection with your sister after she's suggested this . . . incredible sacrifice?" Cecily's voice quavered, partly from outrage, partly from tears.

"What else can it be called when your own sister proposes to have your child . . ." he said, smiling slightly as he patted his wife's hand.

My respect for Peter Kellogg's perception rose several notches. He had unerringly touched one of the difficulties, taken it out, laughed at it and let it be put in its place.

"It'll be *my* child," Cecily said fervently. The terrible childhunger in her face vividly confirmed all that Pat had told me about Cecily's obsession for a child of her own conception. I had seen that look before, in other eyes, and had been unable to bring hope. What if I could bring hope now? And what would happen to Cecily if we failed?

"It won't, of course, draw anything but prenatal nourishment from its host-mother," I said, resorting to the clinical to hide my emotions. "That is—and I cannot stress this strongly enough, Mrs. Kellogg—*if* transplantation is possible. You do realize that's a very big if."

Cecily gave a sigh and then smiled impishly at me. "I know, Dr. Craft. I must not permit myself to hope. But don't you see, hope is so vital an ingredient."

I saw Peter's fingers tighten around her hand, and then he turned to me. "What are the chances?"

"Would you believe one out of four cats?" I couldn't bear the tautness of Cecily's face. "Actually, it works out four to one in rabbits, and with livestock experiments in Texas, a ninety-five percent success with cows and sheep."

"Baaaaa," said Cecily, and again she grinned impishly to show that she was in complete control of herself.

"I've prepared some diagrams, and I've a plan of action to propose," I said, and dug into the bulging briefcase.

Several hours later, we had discussed procedure, probabilities, problems from as many angles as four minds could find. I had explained all the relevant medical procedures, some of which seemed brutal, in the apartment of the prospective parents. My eyes were drawn again and again, unwillingly, to Cecily's oval, delicately flushed face. Despite her continued lightness of word and expression, the hope rekindled was heartbreakingly apparent.

Pat moved to sit beside her brother on the couch. As Peter relied on the verbal descriptions, he leaned back so that the two women could crowd over the diagrams and charts spread over the coffee table. Occasionally he seized his wife's hand to calm her; once, as I explained Pat's role, his other hand gripped his sister's shoulder so tightly that she winced a little. His immense patience and incredible perception made him a good focal point for me, and it was easier to speak to his calm, attentive face than to Cecily's.

He and his wife must have already examined the possibility of exogenesis, or had a superior knowledge of biology, for they showed their familiarity with the principles involved.

"Yes, I can see why cats—maybe; sheep and cows, yes. Let's hope there's more of the bovine in you, darling, than the feline," Peter said, summing up.

"Ha! We'll just blanket the target areas until we succeed. And try and try and try," said Cecily staunchly. "I'm more than willing."

"And that, my darling, is exactly what we have to guard against in you."

"Can you endure the disappointments we're likely to encounter, Cecily?" I asked her bluntly. "In view of your previous medical history," and they all knew I meant psychological, "you will have the hardest task."

"Trust the men to have the easy one," said Cecily, lightly giving a mock angry buffet to Peter's arm.

"That's why we're the superior sex," he said, laughing and pretending to duck from expected blows.

"Even if transplantation is successful," I went on, "you must restrain yourself until such time as you actually hold the child . . ."

"My child . . ."

"In your arms."

"Hey, don't hold your breath," Pat piped up, for that was what Cecily was doing. She laughed sheepishly with the rest of us.

I left Pat with them after making arrangements with Cecily to come to my office for a preliminary pelvic. Then I'd schedule the initial D&Cs for both women.

The warmth of the relationship among the three people,

along with Pat's extraordinary willingness to attempt this im-
probability, warmed me all my cold way home in the frigid
car. I still didn't quite fathom myself caught up in an event as
momentous as this, my abandoned sophomoric dream, might
be. No matter: my routine existence took on a hidden relish as
I became drawn closer and closer to the three amazing people.
Cecily's fervent, oft-repeated "We will! We must!" became my
credo, too.

Those memories were as strong and vivid as the acid interview with Cecily's fashion-plate mother. Night had fallen now,
and my drink was stale. I had another one, stiffer, for courage.

The preliminary steps had gone without a hitch: by a miracle I didn't wish—yet—to subject to too much scientific dissec-
tion, the successful transplantation of the fertilized ovum had
been accomplished by the third attempt. I had fervently
believed that the little plastic film trap would be superior to
any form of flushing, but if it hadn't done the trick the third
time, I would've been forced by Chuck's arguments to try
flushing. Three times he had made the trip across the state to
act as anesthetist at odd early hours in our cottage hospital.

"To think I'm being dictated to by a thermometer's variations," he'd growl.

We were lucky, too, in that there were no questions in the
minds of the hospital administration. Cecily Kellogg had had
three spontaneous abortions within those walls: if she was
willing to keep trying to carry to term, the hospital couldn't
care less—so long as her bills were paid. Pat showed up in the
record as a blood donor. Chuck and I would take Pat home
each time directly she came out of the anesthesia to preserve
the fiction, while Cecily rested on in the ward. At Chuck's in-
sistence, we both kept complete, chronological records of our

procedures, and, for added veracity, punched them in on the staff time clock.

"Remember," he cautioned me more than once, "we will definitely not be able, or want, to keep this a secret. Let's just hope there's no premature slip-up."

I recall groaning at his choice of phrase.

"Sorry about that, Ali. I just shudder to think of the holy medical hell that's going to break loose when this gets out."

"We're not doing anything illegal."

He gave me a patient, forbearing look. "No, we're not, Allison, love. But we are doing something that hasn't been done before, and that is always suspect. I grant you the techniques and theories are pretty well known and understood, but no . . . one . . . has . . . done . . . it on, of all sanctities, the human body." He reverently folded his hands and assumed a pious attitude for a split second. "May I remind you that exogenesis smacks marvelously of the blasphemous?"

"I never considered you to be particularly religious, Chuck."

"Heaven forbid!" He was in one of those contrary moods which could be allowed a man who'd worked a solid day, driven speedily for 250 miles of wearing highway, assisted at some very tricky surgery and, at three-thirty in the morning, had to face a return trip of 250 miles. "You're no longer naive, Ali, but for God's sake just equate the State Senate debates on legalized abortion with what we're doing, and think what will fall on our humbled heads."

"Ah, but we're giving life, not taking it."

"A distinction, but you've got asses who balk at heart massage, resuscitation; you know the furor heart and organ transplants made, to save lives."

"I'm thinking of the hundreds of women who are dying to have kids, who could, by proxy, if this works."

"Great! Great! I'm almost glad you've retained your altruism after—how many years in a small town?" He was disgusted with me. "At least I'm here to set your feet on solid earth once in a while. Now I must into my iron chariot and wend my homeward way. I left my poor overworked partner with the probability of three to five deliveries, one of them almost certain bass-ackward. Before he has a spasm, I hope number three of the G.E. takes. Let me know the minute there's any clinical proof. I will even put you on the short list of those who are permitted to break my slumbers."

He thumped me a little too soundly on the back and departed with a wicked "Fare thee well."

Pat had been a twenty-eight-day regular, almost to the hour, so fifteen days after the third implantation, we held our collective breaths. The next ten days reduced even me to taking tranquilizers. I had to give Cecily the strongest I dared, and I was about to prescribe some for Peter and Wizard. At slightly under four weeks, I gave in and did a pelvic on Pat. The change was definitely apparent. I phoned Chuck. He was in the delivery room, but the nurse promised faithfully to have him call me.

When he rang back, I blurted out the glad news and was taken aback by his total lack of response.

"Sorry, Ali, to sour your big moment," he said so wearily I could almost picture the slump of his lanky body. "Perhaps I'm not as irreligious as I thought. Or perhaps it's just because I delivered a hydrocephalic half an hour ago."

I could sympathize. I'd delivered one as an intern, and it took a long time for me to shake off the shock of that particular abnormality and the illogical sense of guilt I felt, that I had been instrumental in bringing such grief to two perfectly normal, healthy people. Every practicing obstetrician holds his breath as he delivers the child from the womb and unconsciously prays to see the healthy form and condition of a normal baby.

"Maybe we have no right to tamper with conception," Chuck said bitterly. "God knows what we might inadvertently have helped to propagate."

"You know the percentage of spontaneous abortions for damaged or imperfect fetuses . . ."

"Yeah, yeah. I know. But what about damaged cells, blurred chromosomes. . . . And for Christ's sake, Ali, how can we be sure that Pete's sperm fertilizes only Cecily's ovum? I mean, artificial insemination is not as risky as letting those little fellas find their own route up. It could be Pat's that took . . . and then we've got a charming case of consanguinity and a real nasty new batch of genetic problems."

I couldn't say that I hadn't spent some anxious moments worrying about just that. Now I limited my remarks to reminding him that from what we had on Cecily's records of her previous abortions, the fetuses had been in normal growth, with no sign of abnormalities, at the time of abortion; that it was her peculiar uterine construction that interrupted the pregnancies, and not faulty ova. We'd done chromosome checks on all three: never a sign of blurred or damaged cells. But I couldn't argue with him about the virility of Peter's spermatozoa.

"Chuck, you need a stiff drink."

"Sorry to be a wet blanket, Ali, but I guess you do know how I feel, and what I worry about."

"I do. Now get that drink and climb into bed."

"Damned thing's always cold!"

"A condition you ought to have no trouble remedying, Casanova. What about that dulcet-toned nurse of yours?"

"Dulcet tones, yes, but oh, the face!" He was speaking with more of his usual brashness. "I'll spin up there and see the little mother myself soon . . . in the role of a consultant, of course." That's what he said, but his laugh put a different interpretation on the words.

After I hung up, I got to wondering if the Big Time Obstetrician might be interested in Guinea Pig Kellogg. But the idea of Chuck Henderson courting a pregnant virgin overrode my sense of proportion, and I only wished that I could call him back and tease him. I didn't, but I did laugh.

After the initial exultation simmered down, things progressed normally, almost boringly, with Pat's proxy pregnancy. I began to appreciate for the first time why some of my patients bemoaned three-quarters of a year of waiting. Nine months was no longer a matter of ten appointments with one fetal heartbeat, but a damn long stretch.

Peter told me one evening that Cecily was in a constant state of anoxia; she came to me for relief from Dizzy fits. It was not sympathetic pregnancy symptoms with Pat: it was pure and simple anoxia. Mutual friends had begun to remark how radiant Cecily was: one armchair psychiatrist pontificated the opinion that she had finally accepted her childlessness. Then she took up knitting. And took up wearing bulky sweaters and fabrics and bought maternity slacks and skirts.

Pat continued her job as a mathematics teacher in the local high school. Our plan for her to have a sudden emergency leave in the spring did not have to be put into action. She carried almost unnoticeably until the end of the school year, when she was a scant six months. The prevailing fashion of blousy dresses came to our aid, so that her thickening waistline and abdominal bulge were fashionably concealed. One or two unkind friends remarked that she was putting on a little weight, to which she blithely replied that she'd lose it in the summer, before Labor Day. Even if Mrs. Baxter had seen Pat during her brief explosive visit, the pregnancy was barely dis-

cernible. But Cecily, when her mother had phoned her from
the railway station, had thickened her middle with carefully
folded toweling.

Louise Baxter's violent negative reaction shocked both
Peter and Cecily—who had been so happy to tell her mother
the good news. When Peter called me to give warning of my
impending collision with the reluctant grandmother-to-be, I
could hear Cecily sobbing in the background.

There is little point in recounting that explosive interview
from beginning to end. Suffice it to say that Louise Baxter left
me with the distinct impression that her daughter's dearest
wish was an abomination to her. Her agitation was not for my
supposed hoaxing but a genuine—I'll say it—psychotic fear of
ultimate success.

I made a mental note to learn more about the woman from
either Pat or Peter. The one time Pat had made a mildly derog-
atory remark about Louise, Cecily had retorted with an angry
defense. I'd encountered such misplaced loyalty once before
when the mother sweetly dominated her fatherless son into a
psychiatric ward in a catatonic state. With Cecily's emotional
balance under severe stress already, I didn't like to see her loy-
alties torn.

Pat's gestation was calculated to end by August 25. No
baby is late, but even with the date of conception known, there
are possibilities for error. The habits of the Kelloggs suited our
needs to keep the birth unremarkable. They always spent their
vacation months together, usually traveling, and occasionally,
when Peter was working on a book, sequestering themselves in
a quiet upstate village. We hoped for a punctual delivery so
that Pat would be recovered and able to return to school. That
would make fewer waves.

Chuck suggested a small town in the Finger Lake district

which boasted not only a well-equipped hospital but a chief of staff who had been a classmate of ours: Arnold Avery.

Everything was going splendidly, except that Pat did put on more weight than I liked. I didn't suspect a thing, and I can still kick myself that, for all my experience in the field, I could blithely ignore so obvious a clue. Perhaps it was an unwitting desire to discount Chuck's gloomy misgivings. Still, the fetal position was good, the heartbeat strong, about 150. Pat's condition was excellent, and, if she was heavy, she was a fair-sized girl with a good pelvic arch, and a big baby was not unlikely.

However, what was to be known as the Transplantation Split came into existence early the morning of August 15. I'd managed to blackmail a colleague to cover my practice the last three weeks of August and was actually having a non-working vacation in the pleasant company of the Kelloggs. So when Pat woke with abdominal contractions, she roused me to time them. They were a businesslike three minutes apart. It's not unheard of for a primipara to deliver quickly, so I hospitalized her and phoned Chuck to get the hell up there.

If he'd driven instead of hiring that damned helicopter, I'd have been all right. I tell myself, and him when he brings the matter up, as he often does, that I wasn't hogging all the glory for myself. He had a right to some.

At any rate, the helicopter set him down on the hospital grounds just as Pat went into second-stage labor, and he assisted me in the delivery room along with the regular nurse. I hadn't been able to wangle Esther in there, but she was more valuable in the waiting room keeping the parents from exploding.

Chuck and I couldn't restrain our shout of triumph as, at 8:02 A.M., I delivered the six-pound, seven-ounce, perfectly normal, bright red daughter of Peter and Cecily Kellogg from the womb of another woman. I brushed aside the nurse who reached for the newborn and made my own breathless examination of her squalling wrinkled person. I left Chuck to deliver the afterbirth and suture the episiotomy.

"Hey, Doc," Chuck drawled with infuriating irreverence, disrupting my delighted examination, "you forgot something."

Half-angry at his aspersions about my competence, I turned to see him delivering the butt end of another girl child, as healthy as her precipitous sister. I stared transfixed as he eased the head through with deft hands and slapped breath into the mite, who weighed in at a scant five pounds, three ounces.

"You didn't tell me about this," said Chuck, all innocence.

If I'd thought more quickly, I could have told him that I felt he deserved something for all his help.

"I didn't know," I admitted instead.

"God bless you, but I love an honest woman, Ali. It's such a relief."

Then he went over the new girl as carefully as I'd done her sister.

I do feel obliged to add to this account that the heartbeats of identical twins are often synchronized. My mistake lay in assuming a single birth and in not taking a precautionary X ray, as I ordinarily did when the mother appeared to gain more weight than normal or was carrying a large fetus.

My oversight is a family joke, but the most felicitous kind for the Kelloggs. The Transplantation Split is now a familiar medical fact: some minute change in temperature (perhaps moving Pat to my house after the implantation) caused the egg to split, yielding twins. It doesn't always occur in exogenetic pregnancies, but the incidence is proportionately higher than with regular pregnancies.

We were hard put to explain our jubilation to the delivery

room nurse. We made sure that Pat had delivered the afterbirth and would rouse satisfactorily from the anesthesia. Then
we literally burst into the waiting room, simultaneously yelling:

"It's a girl!"

"No, it's—"

"What?" demanded Esther, irritated.

I remember that Cecily looked as if she were about to faint,
but Peter caught on quickly.

"Twins?"

"Ali outdid herself. It's twins!" cried Chuck. "She delivered
your first daughter, a spanking six pounds, seven ounces . . ."

"And I gave Chuck the honor of ushering your second
daughter into the world."

"A very dainty miss at five pounds, three ounces. As
healthy a pair as any parents could wish."

"Pat's all right?" asked Cecily, tears streaming down her
cheeks.

"Right as rain."

"When can we see the children?" asked Peter.

I know I stopped talking and stared at Peter, stunned with
the sad realization that he would never see his children, and
wishing that another miracle would occur for him.

Chuck covered my gaffe. "They'll be in the nursery by
now. Go see the modern product of a virgin birth."

"Dr. Henderson, you ought to be ashamed of yourself," said
Esther, but she wasn't really angry and was far too eager to
see the twins to argue with him.

Champagne is not recommended by any dietitian to break a
night's fast, but we were all back at the vacation cottage, getting pleasantly polluted with toasts to Pat, the parents, Esther,
ourselves, never for a minute suspecting that the hardest part
was just beginning. Not even when the phone rang.

Esther, being nearest, answered it. I just happened to be

looking in her direction, so I saw the abrupt change in her expression and realized that something was wrong. My first thought was for the children, then for Pat. Was she hemorrhaging . . . ?

Esther only listened, openmouthed and sheet-white, and then dazedly put the receiver down.

"Mrs. Baxter's in town," she said, which was sufficient to silence everyone. "A friend of hers saw Peter and Cecily in the supermarket last week and told her. I don't know how she found out about the births . . ."

"We weren't exactly closemouthed about twins," Chuck said, remembering our hilarity when we bought champagne in the town at ten o'clock.

"Well, she went to the hospital, she saw Pat, she saw the twins. She's crazy, the things she said. She told the whole blooming hospital. But it isn't the truth. It isn't the truth at all."

I've never sobered faster in my life. Cecily dashed to the kitchen sink to be ill.

It was a good thing I had medical license plates, because we passed three cops on the way to the hospital at a speed that was unwise even for doctors.

Chuck went for Avery, who was already trying to explain the situation to the village-sheet's reporter who had been informed of this tidbit of malicious gossip. Esther and I dashed to the maternity wing. I could hear Pat's sobbing voice as we turned the corner. I snapped an order for a sedative to the floor supervisor, who made the mistake of not concealing her snide expression.

"Crafty, Crafty," cried Pat as she saw me enter the room. Her two roommates had poisonous expressions on their faces. She was trying to get out of the bed, clutching her tummy. I pushed her back, shoved her legs horizontal and yelled at the nurse to get the hell in there with the hypo.

"Crafty," sobbed Pat in weeping distress, "you can't imagine the horrible things she said. She didn't give me a chance to say anything. I don't think she wanted a logical explanation. She hates Peter! She hates him! She hates Cecily for being so happy with him. And she despises you for giving Cecily her children. I've never seen anyone so full of hate. She must know the children aren't mine and Peter's, but that's what she said. And she kept on saying it, and saying it"—Pat was covering her ears to shut out the sound of that vengeful slander—"and everybody heard it. It's ghastly, Crafty. Oh, Crafty, what will Cecily do?"

I swabbed her arm and gave her the sedative as she was talking—rather, babbling. I also gave orders for her to be moved to a private room. Pat's words became incoherent as the drug took effect. Even as I was pushing her bed toward the private room, I thought of how very characteristic of Pat to worry about Cecily rather than the equivocal position into which Cecily's mother had put herself and her brother. I do not recall ever before being so consumed with anger as I was at that hour in my life. Had I known where Louise Baxter could be found, I think I would have strangled her with my bare hands.

Talk of feathers in the wind, there was no way of stopping the slander. It was obviously all over the hospital and would undoubtedly precede us back into town. I was in such a state of impotent wrath that it was all I could do to keep from lashing out at the floor nurse and the orderly, to wipe the smug expressions from their faces as we shifted Pat.

Pat was mumbling herself into a drugged slumber, and the floor nurse was fussing unnecessarily about the room, when Chuck came stalking through the hall.

"All that fuss because Pat's brother and his wife are helping the girl cover an indiscretion," he said with commendable poise. "What some people will think!" He shook his head over the frailties of mankind and then imperiously gestured the nurse out of the room.

When she'd left he indulged himself in a spate of curses as inventive as they were satisfying, and all relative to the slow and painful demise of one Louise Baxter.

"You've sedated her?" he asked, feeling for Pat's pulse and then stroking her disordered hair back from her face. "Let her sleep."

He turned from the bed and perched his rump against the windowsill, trying to light a cigarette with shaking hands. He finally got it lit and inhaled deeply.

"Is that what you told Avery? That Pat was indiscreet?"

"No, I told him the truth. I've a hunch it might be important later. I can't say he believed me," and Chuck let out a harsh snort of laughter, "but I've convinced him that the charge of—ha!—incestuous fornication is the accusation of a psychotic. He's quite ready to believe that, judging from the way Her Ladyship Baxter carried on. He does think, and he subscribes to making it informally the truth, that we're covering up an illegitimate birth and that Peter and Cecily are going to adopt the children. He's a good man, Avery, but I'm afraid our revolutionary and irreligious fact is beyond his comprehension."

"Illegitimacy is a lot more palatable than"—I couldn't even say it—"the other."

"Our public fiction depends on a cooperative grandmother, and I can't see the likes of her cooperating with either you or me, or the Kelloggs. Christ, how I'd love to get my hands on her. I'd have her committed so fast . . . But Avery will handle matters here—neurotic grandmother, hates to admit her age—

he's smooth as silk. He's having a *long* talk with that floor supervisor—one for letting Baxter in, two for not shutting her up the moment she started, and three for half-believing her." He walked back to Pat, feeling her abdomen.

"No, it's hard," I said.

"I'd like to move her out of here, quickly."

"Will Avery let Esther stay on as special?" I asked.

"You just bet he will," said Esther from the door, grim-lipped. She was in her whites, starched and ready for action. I was inordinately relieved. "What else do you expect from provincial hospitals?" She checked Pat, smoothed the bed-clothes unnecessarily and began checking the room's equipment, as if she hoped to find fault with it. "They don't have rooming in or I'd bring the babies right here. But she's all right with me. You'd better get back to the cottage. Oh, and Doc-tor Craft, I administered a strong sedative to Cecily before I came out. You look as if you need one, too, Allison," she added and then settled herself on the chair by the sleeping Pat.

As we passed Avery's office on the way out, we heard him administering quite a lecture to some unfortunate person.

Wizard's angry barking alerted us before we turned off the main road into the lane that led to the cottage. Two of the group hovering by the path evidently had urgent business somewhere else.

"My God! People! I hate 'em," muttered Chuck, staring bel-ligerently back at the four hangers-on as we parked the car.

"Don't go in there," one of the men told Chuck. "That dog's dangerous!"

"Is he?" asked Chuck with innocent mildness, and we walked right past the snarling dog.

"Howd'ya like that?" someone muttered.

Peter was in the shadows of the small screened porch.

"Esther gave Cecily something. She'd made herself ill with weeping," he said. "Is Pat all right?"

"Esther's with her. Avery's handling the hospital staff." Chuck wearily combed his hair back from his forehead. "He doesn't believe in exogenesis, but the notion that you and Cecily are going to adopt your sister's indiscretion is acceptable."

"What?"

Perhaps it was a trick of the sun, but I thought I saw a glint of anger in Peter's dead eyes.

"How long do Pat and the babies have to stay here?"

"We'll leave as soon as Pat can stand the trip," I said, sagging against the wall.

Chuck sort of maneuvered me into the nearest chair, but it faced the pathway and the curious faces parading by. I tried to tell myself it was reaction to the whole nasty scene, but I was depressed by the notion that if Louise Baxter had spread her filth this fast in a small vacation village, she'd sure as hell go on to pollute the more rewarding atmosphere of our university town. Though what she stood to gain by such slander, I couldn't understand.

Before we all got very drunk, Chuck sat me down at the dining room table, and we wrote up our notes on the delivery. I could see that they were going to be very important documents, but the clinical reportage sure as hell took the glamour out of the achievement, just as surely as Louise Baxter had tarnished the greatest gift of love.

The third day after her delivery, we took Pat and the babies home downstate in an ambulance. As I was still nominally on my vacation and I certainly didn't want Pat alone in her apartment in her psychological condition, I insisted that she stay in my house. So Chuck, who was following the ambulance in my station wagon, turned off to go to Pat's apartment to pick up a list of unmaternity clothing for her. Peter, Cecily, Wizard and the babies dropped out of the cavalcade for their place.

Esther and I had just suitably settled Pat when first Chuck, brakes squealing viciously, then Cecily and company pulled up in my driveway.

I had thought in the hospital three days earlier that Chuck had a superb vocabulary of invective, but he had evidently kept a supply in reserve which he now employed as he helped Peter out of the car with the babies.

"What happened?" I asked, rather inanely, because it took little guessing.

"That blankety-blank female is not going to have an incestuous woman living in her respectable house. And to think that she had once admired her. And to think that all along that adulterous woman had been poisoning the minds of helpless youngsters and— Do I really need to read further from that script?" asked Chuck, now at the top of his strong baritone voice. He woke young Anne Kellogg.

"Mrs. Baxter's got to town?"

"Quod erat demonstrandum! Only I'd say that the bitch has *gone* to town!" Incongruously, Chuck was deftly soothing the frightened baby before he passed her on to Esther.

Peter's usually calm face was etched with grief as he helped Cecily up the steps. Wizard, head down, tail limp, followed them to the steps, then turned and settled himself on the paving, watching the front gate.

"We are no longer welcomed by the management of the apartment house," was all Peter said.

"Good Lord," said Esther, "did she use a bullhorn?"

Then the phone rang. Jiggling Anne, Esther answered it. She listened for a moment, then with grave pleasure firmly replaced the handset.

"I think it would be better to have the phone disconnected or the number changed immediately, Dr. Craft. Shall I put in the request?"

I nodded numbly.

Wizard uttered a warning bark, and Chuck peered out the window.

"Who're they?" he asked me, and I glanced out at three militant figures about to enter the yard.

I shook my head.

"Peter, is Wizard on the guard?"

Peter nodded sadly. So we watched as the trio opened the gate. Wizard advanced menacingly, slowly, but his intention was quite plain. The visitors hesitated, conferred together, withdrew. Wizard took up a new position, twenty yards from the gate.

In the next few hours I would not have traded Wizard's presence for a cordon of unpolluted police. An irate mob might charge a police line (I don't say we had the quantities of a mob), but our visitors had not the courage to face 125 pounds of belligerent unleashed German shepherd. It was incredible to me, or maybe just naive of me, that so many people could believe such a thing of Pat and Peter Kellogg, but the traffic past my house was inordinately heavy. I like to think that those who paused and were not growled at by Wizard had friendly intentions, but they were very few. I still can't figure out why people have to descend in such mobs on the unusual.

At any rate, the only one who entered the house until the police came was the telephone man, and he wouldn't pass the gate until Peter had snapped the choke-chain lead on Wizard.

I frankly don't remember much of the next few hours. I think we all sat around in a semi-stupor, with the exception of the practical Esther. We had brought some of the food left over in the cottage, but it wasn't enough, and more formula mixture was needed, so Esther went out . . . the back way. She returned shortly afterward and grumbled angrily under her breath the entire time she cooked lunch, though I don't know what it was she served us. Fortunately there were lusty, hungry, healthy babies to care for, and I think they saved our sanity. If I heard Chuck mutter it once, I heard it fifty times:

"We got the kids!"

With Wizard to guard the house, none of us paid any attention to our whilom visitors or hecklers until we heard the police siren whine down to inaudibility right outside the house.

"Well, they took their time," said Esther with righteous indignation.

Innocently we all filed out onto the porch. Wizard was impartial enough to resent police intrusion.

"Call off the dog. We're on official business," the first man ordered.

Wizard obediently retreated to Peter's side at command.

"You certainly took your time coming," Esther said acidly. "We've been plagued by . . ."

"Which one of you is Peter Kellogg?" the policeman interrupted her arrogantly.

Peter raised his hand.

"I have a warrant for your arrest. Incestuous fornication and adultery is a crime in this state, buddy." There was no doubt of his private opinion of such an offense. "Which of you women is Patricia Kellogg? I've got a warrant for her arrest on the same charge."

Chuck snatched the second warrant out of the cop's hand. When the policeman stepped forward to retrieve it, Wizard gave a warning snarl. Chuck read the document hastily.

"Christ! It is in order, Peter." Chuck had been angry before; now he looked defeated.

"Can't he read his own, mister?" sneered one of the cops.

The other man jabbed him in the ribs and pointed to the dog.

"As you perfectly well know, Joseph Craig," Esther replied, her fury so plain that Policeman Joseph Craig stepped back, "Professor Kellogg was blinded in Vietnam."

"I'm Dr. Henderson, Miss Kellogg's physician. I cannot permit her to answer this summons in person. She's under heavy sedation and incapable of supporting any additional strain."

"You can come with me then, Doctor, and tell it to the judge." Then the man informed Peter of his rights and gestured him off the porch.

Chuck turned to me. "Call"—he gave me a number—"and ask for Jasper Johnson and get him to work immediately."

"Hey, that dog can't come," the arresting officer complained, backing hurriedly away from Wizard's path.

"He's Professor Kellogg's seeing-eye dog, and he . . ."

"Hell, he won't need any eyes where he's going!"

"Wizard had better stay here, Chuck," Peter said with quiet meaning. He bent down and cradled the dog's head in his hands. Wizard whined quizzically as if he already understood. Hard not to, with the atmosphere crackling with suppressed emotions.

"Wizard, guard Cecily. Guard the babies. Obey Crafty. Understand?"

Wizard whined, sneezed, and bowed his head but made no move to follow Peter, Chuck and the policemen. But the moment some of the bystanders tried to crowd in at the gate, he renewed his vigilance with savage growls and risen hackles.

It seemed to take forever to get Johnson's number, and then they must have done an office-to-office search for this Jasper Johnson before his brisk voice came on the line. I explained the situation as tersely as possible.

"For this I joined a fraternity ten years ago?" was his cryptic comment; then I heard him mmm-ing to himself for a moment or two. "For such extraordinary charges I'd better get up there. They have to accept bail, but I can do that by phone. I should be able to make it to your place in about two hours at this time of day." Then he groaned. "But my wife's going to hate me again."

His flippancy was oddly reassuring, and as I cradled the phone, the awful depression began to lift.

Chuck and Peter came home in a taxi about an hour later.

"Under the circumstances, I'm sure the neighbors would have preferred another four-alarm fanfare," Chuck said snidely as they came up the walk.

"You're forgetting what Sergeant Weyman said," Peter remarked.

"Yeah," and Chuck's expression brightened.

"George Weyman better be on our side," said Esther, her eyes blazing. "After all Allison did to save his wife and baby. So what did George say?"

"That this was the biggest load of shit he'd ever seen made official," said Peter with a grin.

"He read the riot act to Craig and his cohort and treated us with more courtesy than is customary in police routines. However, I can't be as charitable about His Honor."

"Who?" asked Esther.

"Colston."

That didn't surprise either of us.

"I assume by virtue of our speedy release on bail that you contacted Jasper. Is he coming up?"

"He gave himself two hours."

"Two hours? Well, I suppose he has to obey speed limits. He's only got a Mercury, poor deprived lad." Chuck gave one of his wicked laughs. "His last three babies paid for my Lincoln." His amusement faded, and he barged toward the kitchen. "I need a drink. We all need a drink to celebrate this third day P.P.E."

"P.P.E.?" asked Peter.

"Yeah," Chuck called from the kitchen, where he was rattling bottles and glasses. He came back in with a laden tray. "Postpartum exogenesis."

Conversation lagged, and Peter, Chuck, Esther and I sipped our drinks fairly meditatively. I knew I was trying to numb my perceptions even while I knew that drinking at this pace wouldn't do the trick. Then one of the babies started crying and just as suddenly stopped. Pat wandered in from the kitchen with Carla and a bottle.

"Hey," Chuck said, ushering her to a seat, "you shouldn't be awake yet."

Pat shrugged indifferently and settled the baby in the crook of her arm, smiling as her hungry wail was cut off by the nipple.

"I see that my job doesn't end with producing them," she said. "Funny thing. You know, Crafty, I miss their kicking. I waited for it as I was waking up, and I got a little panicky when I didn't feel it, and then I remembered I'd had the babies." Her tender reminiscent smile faded abruptly. "Ah, well. Good thing I'm their aunt, I can tell you. I'd just hate to have to give up all title to them."

Chuck and I exchanged worried frowns over her bent head. In all the unpleasantness I'd forgotten about the emotional impact of maternity on Pat. She was a mother, and she wasn't. She had had all the emotional, biological and psychological distortion of pregnancy, and if the problem was not handled carefully, her involvement could become critical. In the ill-wind department, perhaps this flap would provide sufficient, if salacious, distraction, and she might be damned glad—both psychologically and emotionally—to be relieved of any relationship with the two kids she'd borne.

"Let me hear you say that in another week of sleep-torn nights, m'dear," said Chuck wryly. The twins had different internal clocks.

"Ha," Pat said with some disgust. "With all the professional help around here, you have to have a priority rating to get close to one of them."

Peter moved over to the couch to sit beside her. He touched the child's head where it rested on her arm, cupping the downy scalp in his big hand, his thumb hovering over the fontanel and its gentle pulse. With fingertips, he "read" Carla's face and one waggling arm.

"There are advantages to being blind. I can truthfully say to Cecily that she grows not a day older." Peter smiled gently. "She's truthful, too, and tells me of her wrinkles and graying hair, but I don't see them, any more than I can see the changes they say have occurred all around me. Visual time has stopped forever for me, and I 'see' only my memories." His hand cupped the warm little head. "I've seen a lot of babies. I know what one usually looks like . . ." What he didn't say was palpable in the room. Esther wasn't the only one who made hurried use of a kleenex.

Chuck cleared his throat and remarked with a broad professional pomposity, "I assure you, sir, your daughter is most beautiful for one so newly born, which, truthfully, isn't very beautiful. She *is* losing the lobster shade of red, her chin *has* come forward, the head bones are gradually assuming a normal . . ."

"Charles Henderson, how can you?" cried Pat, outraged. "Carla is a perfectly beautiful child. Ignore this clinical lout, Peter. He's just plain jealous."

"Truer word was never spoken," Chuck said in a doleful tone.

"Couldn't you have made an honest woman out of any of

them," I asked, plaintively, "and acknowledged a child or two?"

Chuck negligently waved aside my suggestion of wholesale philandering. "A baby for A, a baby for B, but never, oh never, a baby for me," he warbled slightly off pitch.

"Oh, you mean, 'always the deliverer, never the delivered'?" asked Pat, all innocence as she deftly burped Carla over one shoulder.

"You can say that about Ali here, not me," said Chuck with simulated indignation.

"Thank heavens you're here," said a voice at the door. "I got home only half an hour ago, and your number doesn't seem to ring."

We all turned.

"Dr. Dickson!" cried Peter, rising to his feet, since he had identified the voice before we could turn to see who could possibly have got past Wizard. "Trust that dog to know our friends."

"Indeed, indeed. Wizard and I are the best of good friends. Such a magnificent beast, such intelligence, such sympathy. I wish I could get along as well with some of the human members of my congregation as I do with Wiz."

Peregrine Dickson, the minister of my Presbyterian church, entered the room, simultaneously mopping a perspiring face and shaking each of our hands with a warm but firm grip. He was a medium-sized, middle-aged, slightly overweight, slightly balding man, but only his physical appearance was mediocre or slight. His whole personality exuded inexhaustible good humor, patience and empathy, and his kindly face, with alert twinkling eyes, was well wrinkled with laugh lines.

"My dear Peter, how happy I am for you! Allison, my dear girl, but I'd expect you to help!" He shook my hand, passed on to Esther, and grasped Chuck's hand so that I had to make an introduction instead of an explanation. Then Perry Dickson was bending over Carla. "What a remarkably handsome baby! Her sister sleeps? Twins! Well, my word, my smart Pat never does things by halves, does she? I always like to baptize twins. I feel it puts me ahead two steps in the Good Book instead of the usual one. But what an extraordinary resemblance," and he paused, backing off slightly from Carla and narrowing his eyes much as a painter does for perspective. He looked at Pat with an expression akin to awe. "However did you manage that, Pat? But bless you for carrying through with it and giving Peter and Cecily the children. Is Cecily resting?" He looked about hopefully and then collapsed beside Pat on the sofa, mopping his sweating face with his limp handkerchief. "I shouldn't wonder. Such a hot, close day."

At that point Esther appeared with a glass of lemonade for him.

"Thank you, Esther. You are always beforehand. Really, it seems as if I've been hurrying for hours. It's a relief to get here and sit!" Dr. Dickson took a sip or two and then put his glass down to continue his monologue. "I was overcome with joy for you, Peter, when I heard the news. After all, I did baptize you, did confirm you, did marry you, and now I shall be able to start that comforting cycle with the new generation . . ."

Perry Dickson could rattle on so engagingly that you didn't have time to organize your own thoughts or rebuttals. I was beginning to realize that Perry was telling Peter that the irregularity of the children's births would be no bar to their admission in church.

"Perry," I tried to get a word in edgewise, "I don't think you've heard what . . ."

"Tut, Allison, I hear everything, you know. Someone always tells *me*. As I'm a minister, there is always something they think I should hear. That may be one reason why I am impelled to talk so much, so no one else will have a chance to tell me something they *think* I ought to know.

"In this instance, a kind parishioner—she is very charitable . . . with her purse—actually telephoned me at the Retreat House with such an exceptional interpretation of a really unexceptional occurrence," and he smiled sweetly at Pat, "that I realized I had better return forthwith. I was already packed when Father Ryan phoned."

"Father Ryan?" Peter and I exclaimed together.

Beside me, Chuck shuddered, groaned, and covered his eyes with his hand. "We're in trouble with the ecclesiastical as well as the secular?"

"Oh, I hardly think so. I assure you, Father Ryan gave me no details, but he was so emphatic that I return because of the . . . tone . . . of the gossip . . ." And now Perry Dickson faltered, as though in the rush the truth had not had a chance to catch up with him. He looked blankly at me, only I didn't know how to start.

"Then you do not believe, Dr. Dickson," Peter asked deliberately, "that the children are mine and Pat's?"

"Good heavens, no!" Perry Dickson lifted voice, eyes and hands upward in horrified repudiation of the thought. Then he gave Pat the kindest possible smile. "I can only hope, Patricia, that you weren't indiscreet just to give Peter and Cecily the child they've longed for."

"He simply hasn't tumbled," said Chuck to the rest of us, almost annoyed.

"I haven't what?" and Perry looked at the solid sofa as if it were expected to collapse under him.

"Pat was not indiscreet, Dr. Dickson," said Peter in his quietly emphatic way. "She is not an illegitimate mother. She acted as the host-mother for Cecily's and my progeny." And he gestured toward Chuck and me.

"She was . . . the . . . host? Mother?" Perry's face was absolutely still. He held his breath while the words made sense to him. He blinked his eyes once, twice, and then gave such a triumphant crow that Carla jerked partially awake and whimpered. "Exogenesis?" His eyes went so wide that his brows joined his receding hairline. "Exogenesis!" He grabbed at Chuck for reassurance, and, grinning, Chuck nodded vigorously.

"Exogenesis documented and done!"

"Exogenesis! Exogenesis!" Perry said in wild excitement. "Oh, absolutely magnificent. Patricia! My dear girl, greater love hath no woman! My dear child!" He was embracing her in an excess of emotion. He pumped Chuck's hand, grabbed Peter in an exultant hug, all the while mumbling "exogenesis" in every sort of tone, from excited, incredulous and relieved to prayerful.

While we were still grinning delightedly at the effect of our revelation on the good doctor, he collapsed again on the sofa, fanning himself with the soaked handkerchief. "Oh, my dear people, my dear, dear friends . . ." Then he clapped his hands together and stared down at Carla. "Well, that would, of course, explain it. Wouldn't it?" Then another thought struck his reeling brain. "Oh, good heavens, poor Father Ryan!" At that exclamation, Chuck started to howl with laughter. "Whatever will *he* say? Oh, my word!" There was, however, an unholy look of gleeful anticipation in Perry's eyes despite the humble dismay in his voice. "This is going to strike him at a very fundamental point in his dogma. However is he going to explain this away? Oh, my dear friends, how could you?" As if we'd achieved only to discomfort Father Ryan.

"I'd be glad to provide you with the records," Chuck said, and then took a wild look at Pat but obviously could not restrain himself, "because they prove that it's an undisputable virgin birth! My dear Patricia, I could not resist!"

We all pounced on Chuck for that, while he kept demanding what was wrong with the guys in this burg and begging Pat's forgiveness. She was so torn between laughter and embarrassment that she couldn't say a thing, but the general confusion roused the baby in her arms. She made that an excuse to leave the room, saying that the conversation had taken a damned crude turn for her virgin ears and it was not fit talk for her niece's impressionable mind.

When we had calmed down, wiping the tears of mirth from our cheeks—we had needed that laugh—Perry pressed us for details. We had no hesitation in being candid with him: it was to our advantage.

"To go back a bit," he suggested when he'd absorbed the important facts and points of the exogenetic technique, "you said something about being in trouble with the ecclesiastical as well as the secular. Now, exactly what did you mean?"

"Your kind parishioners didn't have all the news, Dr. Dickson," said Chuck. "Warrants were served on Peter and Pat about two hours ago for incestuous fornication and adultery."

Perry's eyes went out of focus, and his jaw dropped.

"Oh, my word! How terrible! I mean, who would possibly . . ."

"My mother," said Cecily from the hall door. She was pale but composed. Pat came in behind her.

Dr. Dickson was on his feet instantly, and after giving her the gentlest, most affectionate of embraces, he drew her and Pat back to the couch to sit on either side of him. He was patting their hands consolingly.

"My dear child, are you *positive* it was Louise?"

"Oh, yes," Pat answered. "Mrs. Baxter visited the cottage hospital where I was registered as Cecily Kellogg . . . so the birth certificate would show the real parents. It was Louise."

"I have never understood your mother's antagonism toward Peter," Perry said to Cecily, "particularly since he is so like your own dear father, but for her to . . . to scandalize her own daughter. . . . I shudder!"

Cecily was doing just that, and then Wizard's warning bark caught her and us up short.

"Hey, call off this dog before I have to shoot him!" yelled an irate male voice.

We looked out the front windows. A police car, without sirens, had pulled up to the curb behind an equally official looking white station wagon. I couldn't see the emblem on its side, but there was a uniformed nurse sitting on the passenger side. The policemen were in their car, just watching the perspiring seersucker-suited man held at bay by Wizard.

"You oughta tie up a vicious animal like that," he said to me as Peter and I got to the porch ahead of the others.

"The shepherd is there to keep off trespassers," I told the man.

"Well, I ain't trespassing. I'm on official business."

"What kind?" asked Chuck, solidly planting himself in the doorway.

"Call off that dog first."

"Only after you state your business."

Dr. Dickson tugged at Chuck's sleeve but kept back in the shadow of the doorway.

"He's a process server," Perry whispered. "I don't usually interfere with the grinding of legal wheels, but stall him!"

"Why?" Pat asked in an urgent low voice.

Perry pulled her back into the house, and out of the corner of my eye I saw Cecily join them and disappear down the hall. Then my attention was engaged by this latest emissary of law and order.

"Look, call off that dog. I got a court order here to take into protective custody the infants"—he turned the paper right-side up so he could read it—"Carla and Anne Kellogg."

Peter groaned, his shoulders sagging hopelessly. Chuck threw a protecting arm about him.

"You'll never take those children from me," Peter said in low but distinct tones.

"Buddy, you gonna be in contempt of court, too?" He beckoned toward the police car, and the officers got out and ranged themselves behind him.

"Mr. Kellogg, you better give up those kids, unless you want to be in more trouble than you already are," one of them advised. "I'd hate like hell to shoot Wizard, but you're resisting a court order."

"Issued by whom?" demanded Peter.

"That don't matter, Mr. Kellogg. We got a writ for the kids, and we're gonna have to take 'em."

"Oh, really?" asked a suave voice cheerfully.

"Jasper, thank God," cried Chuck, leaping off the porch to greet the tall, excessively thin man turning in at the gate. We had been so engrossed with the threat of the process server that we hadn't noticed the sleek black Mercury convertible pull up to the curb. "Legal eagle, do your stuff, now if ever!"

Jasper held out an array of long white bones and snapped them negligently for the warrant, which he examined very closely, whistling as he handed it back.

"'Fraid it's all too legal and binding, folks," he said dolefully, and, grabbing Chuck by the arm, he propelled him past Wizard to gather us into a conference group on the porch.

The process server tried to follow, only to stare at bared teeth. The policeman stepped forward, too, his hand on his revolver butt.

"For God's sake, man, I must confer with my clients," said Jasper, waving peremptorily at them to keep their distance.

"Let them proceed. Let them search the house," he told us in a low voice. "Oh, it's all right. I know what I'm doing," he said at our shocked reactions. "Someone control that dog, huh?"

Reluctantly, Peter called Wizard to him. The dog's whining protest echoed my feelings precisely as we numbly watched the odious little man enter the house and trudge toward the hall.

"You've some powerful enemies, to get that kind of writ served so damned quick," Jasper said to us sotto voce.

"Goddammit, Johnson," Chuck said, but at that moment the process server came storming back into the living room, holding up an empty carry cot.

"Where are they? I saw a woman holding a baby when I drove up here. Now where are they?"

"Where are who?" asked Pat as she and Cecily came in from the kitchen. "Who's this? What's he doing storming around here?" Pat sounded quite indignant.

"Where are those babies? I got a writ!"

"There are no babies in this house," said Cecily quietly. "Go ahead, look!"

"There were babies!" The empty carry cot was brandished and then flung onto the couch.

"How the hell did you do that?" Chuck muttered to Jasper, and then all of us had to keep our questions and our emotions to ourselves, for the process server came charging back into the room.

"I want those kids. Where are they?"

"You'll have a stroke, rushing around like this in all the heat," Chuck said dispassionately.

"Mr. Kellogg, you're in enough trouble," one of the cops said.

"I'll get those kids, you incestuous bast—"

Peter's fist was cocked, but Chuck was quicker. His punch landed with a satisfactory crunch that sent the process server toppling over the sofa arm, onto the edge of the carry cot, which tipped onto his head, smothering him briefly in, I hoped, smelly sheeting.

"That's assault, mister," one of the cops said severely, and started for Chuck. Wizard crouched, growling.

"With four impartial witnesses to testify to undue provocation?" asked Jasper. "I think not." The crispness and authority in Jasper's manner cooled the situation. He gestured to the policeman to help the groaning man to his feet, at which point Jasper relieved him of the piece of paper he was still clutching. "You are only required to serve the court's warrants, summons and writs, in a manner befitting the dignity of your position, which does not include slanderous remarks."

"As there are no babies, infants, kids on these premises, Officer, I suggest you search elsewhere." He handed back the summons.

The two policemen and the server conferred briefly and, after hovering for a few minutes indecisively, finally left, Wizard hurrying their gateward way.

The moment they were out of earshot, we turned on the girls for an explanation. Pat was grinning triumphantly, but Cecily was gravely sad.

"Peregrine Dickson spirited them out the back door, muttering something about the instruments of the Lord, divine timing, the FBI and his conscience," Pat told us. "If you could have seen him, trailing receiving blankets, the bag of formula bounding on his hip, ducking through the garden . . ." and she covered her mouth to smother her laughter.

"That was the sight I caught as I drove around the corner," said Jasper, smiling as broadly.

"I apologize for all my recent foul thoughts, Jasper," said Chuck earnestly. "I was afraid that when Ed cured you of your last ulcer, he'd also removed the milk of human kindness from your scrawny breast."

Jasper shuddered. "For God's sake, Chuck, don't mention milk again," and he made a show of retching. "Now, which is which of you two charming ladies? I can't tell the real mother without an introduction, and, frankly, you both look like death warmed over."

"Best lawyer in the world!" said Chuck. "Always tells the truth!"

"I'm Cecily Kellogg," Cecily said, shaking Jasper's hand warmly, "and if you can do anything to keep them from taking my children away from me . . ."

"I've already made myself an accessory after the fact, my dear Mrs. Kellogg, though I must confess I never suspected they'd move that far this fast. It's a rare instance that the children are removed from the care of their parents until actual guilt is established. Even then, the state hesitates. The worst parent is considered preferable to none at all. I'd say that whoever's after you has some very influential friends."

"It's Mother, then," said Cecily, sinking to the sofa as if her legs had given way. Peter reached for and found her hands and held them firmly.

"Your mother?" Jasper's urbane manner was briefly shattered.

"Mother has always managed to have influential friends, and she's always used them whenever necessary."

"She's ruthless," Chuck said.

"Ra-ther," replied Jasper.

"And psychotic as all hell."

"Obviously. Therefore twice as dangerous." Jasper spun on his heel, one hand shoved into his pocket, the other absently smoothing down the hair across the back of his head as he paced. "Dr. Craft gave me a splendid outline, but now I want full details, please."

While we recounted the events of the last year, he continuously paced, apologizing at one point by saying the walking helped him concentrate. I was later to be amazed at the accuracy of his total recall. When we had given him the whole story, he made one more complete circuit and halted in front of the couch, looking down at Peter and Cecily.

"The action against you revolves around a morality charge."

"'Incestuous fornication is against the law in this state, buddy,'" repeated Chuck.

"Yes, it is," Jasper said, "but d'you know, I had to look it up?" He smoothed his hair again. "You sure picked a dilly. Did you have to be related to him?" he asked Pat in a petulant tone.

"It's not at all the thing you do for total strangers," she replied blandly.

"So we disprove the moral issue, also the consanguinity—although how they hoped to remedy *that* by depriving you of the children, I can't guess, and the charge must, by definition, be dropped."

"The *charge*, yes," said Pat gloomily. "But how about the slander?" and she gestured toward the front of the house.

"Yes," and Jasper heaved a sigh. "I don't suppose you object to the procedures becoming public knowledge?" he asked me.

"Exogenesis will have to be admitted into the record—even though it will mean that hordes of childless women will descend on Ali," Chuck replied before I could answer.

"Well, they'd be preferable to sensation-seekers," I said.

"True, true. We shall have to bide our time," Jasper said

gently, apologetically, "before we spring that explanation, so I'm afraid you all will remain under an unenviable cloud for a bit. Did you keep medical records of this medical tour de force?"

"By God, we did—every temperature drop, every miligram of medication," said Chuck.

"They can be admitted as evidence."

"Even from prejudiced sources?" I asked. "I expect I'm considered one of your accessories to facts, too."

"And me? Don't forget me," said Chuck belligerently.

"Or me," spoke up Esther, her jaw set as determinedly.

"Oh, you're all so wonderful," said Cecily, and then dissolved into tears, apologizing through hiccuping sobs. Chuck exchanged looks with me, but Cecily refused sedation and pulled herself together.

"I'm sorry to seem callous or brutal, Mrs. Kellogg, but I've always operated on a completely candid basis with my clients. I can, however, promise you that I can move for an emergency hearing on this. I'm not without a few influential friends myself. Now, to resume. Medical records, Dr. Craft, no matter the source, are considered reliable information by the court. The hospital where the twins were born, your own institution here, will certainly have corroborative records?" We nodded, and he said he could subpoena them. "Now, I'll need the blood types of the three principals and the children. That should prove conclusively whose children they are, shouldn't it?"

Chuck caught my dubious glance and shrugged.

"Well, won't it?" Jasper asked. "In paternity cases, I know . . ."

"Man, this is a *ma*ternity case," Chuck said.

"Yes, but . . ."

"Blood types only prove that the person could or could not be the parent, not that he or she *is*."

"Yes, but . . ."

"In fact, since we are being brutally frank, and damn well have to be," Chuck went on grimly, "until we know what the twins' types are, we don't actually know that Pat couldn't be the mother."

Pat gasped, and Cecily snuggled closer to Peter, hiding her head in his shoulder.

"You mean, that awful charge that I had my brother's children could be true?"

"Wait a minute, Pat," and Chuck reached across the coffee table to hold her down on the sofa. *"Not* by incestuous fornication, however. The medical records absolve you of the morality charge right there. But, God damn it, it is possible—not probable"—he paused to let his emphasis sink in—"that the active sperm of the father could have fertilized ova of both the intended mother *and* the carrier."

"The twins are *identical*," I reminded Chuck as well as the others.

"True, so they both came from one fertilized ovum. Both Ali and I have worried about that *possibility* . . ."

"And I had twins . . ." breathed Pat, horrified.

"No, no, Pat, you've missed the point. You and Peter are fraternal twins, two eggs fertilized at the same time. This is an egg split, an entirely different process. And to keep you from turning neurotic, with such a close linkage, genetically speaking, it is unlikely you'd have had such healthy kids. Inbreeding multiplies defective and recessive genes, and an inbred child generally shows visible proof of the problem—frailness, sickliness. Those kids are beautiful, perfect, healthy."

"Look," began Jasper authoritatively, and something in his attitude gave Pat and Cecily reassurance, "it doesn't take long to have blood types tested, so we can take you three off that particular tenterhook pretty quickly. Okay? So tell me how to get in touch with our clerical kidnapper. By the way, I'm sorry to have to advise you that it is better that you don't know where the children have been taken. I do promise that I'll do everything I can to see that you have them back in a very short time."

I gave him Dr. Dickson's home address, and he glanced around the room.

"I wish I had met you people under slightly happier circumstances, but let me say that it'll be my pleasure to represent you. By God, exogenesis!" His eyes held the same stunned, incredulous expression that Perry Dickson's had. "Wait till the Catholic Church gets hold of this one."

"In a sense, it has," Dr. Dickson said from the doorway. He had a new handkerchief, which he used as vigorously on his face as he had the other. "When I returned . . . well, from where I went"—he smiled at Jasper as the lawyer quickly gestured to him not to be specific—"Father Ryan had called. I haven't seen the poor man so distressed since the day we both arrived to preach a burial service over the same grave. It was a grisly joke, because the man had been an atheist of the most vehement sort . . . a fact we both knew. His relatives—tsk, tsk, terrible people; no wonder he was an atheist. I digress, a fault I cannot correct even when I'm not sermonizing . . .

"Father Ryan, yes. He had heard of the incredible charges being made against the Kelloggs, and he wished to know if there was any way in which he could help . . ."

"Father Ryan?" Peter asked, surprised and, I could see, rather gratified.

"Oh, yes. Father Ryan has the highest regard for you, Peter. His exact words were, 'There is nothing Byronic about that young man in his poems or his personality.' So! There! He is quite willing to testify to your moral fiber if his presence would be of any help. Indeed, he insists on it."

"Does he know about the exogenetic twist?" asked Peter with wry humor.

"Well, as to that, I'm afraid to . . . Peter, I just couldn't tell him yet." It was the first time I'd known Perry Dickson to be at a loss for words. "Just think, Peter, this renders a major, an essential, Catholic mystery a mere surgical technique. But you know, it has occurred to me that such a possibility merely enlarges the mystery rather than explodes it." The handkerchief was flourished to provide the appropriate gestures. "For was not our Lord Jesus remarkable because of the person He was, not just because of His holy origin? And surely, does not such a miraculous method of arousing our instincts for good give evidence to even the most confirmed unbeliever that there is an agency, a being—God, who *does* care and who directs our petty ways?

"Oh, my oh my, and this is only Tuesday. At all events, the babies are safely bestowed"—and his face was painfully earnest —"where, I assure you, they will have the most loving and competent care, and," he went on more briskly, mopping his forehead, "complete anonymity." He sighed. "Poor Father Ryan. But I did do right in spiriting the children away, didn't I?"

"Morally, yes," Jasper said. "Legally, no. If you hadn't, I should have tried to snatch them myself." He looked at us. "I realized what was up when I saw the nurse in the Red Cross wagon. And you know how I prefer to operate, Chuck: strictly on the up-and-up."

"I sometimes suspect that the up-and-up has a little bit of down in it in the middle," remarked the minister. "Now what's to be done?"

Jasper explained about the necessity for blood tests.

"Oh, I don't see that that will matter," Perry said. "However, for the legal minds, one must produce documents. But it won't, in the final analysis, matter if the blood types *are* similar."

"Why on earth not?" demanded Jasper, surprised.

"You doctors and lawyers consider legal and scientific proof the only essentials, but I fear you forget the power of human conceit. All those weighty clinical and notarized statements look most imposing on the record, and show that the lawyer has been worthy of his hire. Indeed, this sort of event needs all the documentation possible. But have no fears." He rose to his feet, gesturing. "All is resolved for the righteous. Vengeance is mine, saith the Lord. It's unchristian of me, I know, but such justice, such divine justice . . . No, I digress again. Mr. Johnson, if you'll just come with me, we can settle the matter of blood types from the children, and then I shall have to be about other of my Father's business. Old Mrs. Rothman, you know . . ."

He had bustled Jasper out of the house like a dinghy pushing a sleek yacht.

"I wonder how Father Ryan will take the news," said Peter as he stroked Wizard's head.

Jasper was as good as his word about obtaining an emergency hearing with the Juvenile Court. He did remark that he had no opposition from the prosecution. He had commented again on the influence of our enemy's friends because the State of New York was the complainant, not an individual.

"Of course, the sovereign State of New York *is* the guardian of all children within its borders, but it's a neat piece of legal eagling."

It was good to know that our ordeal had limits, because the

atmosphere in town was, to use the so apt teen-age phrase, "hairy."

"Sure takes a moral crisis to tell the sheep from the goats," Esther remarked as she scratched off another patient from my books. "Just as well; McCluskey, Derwent, Patterson and Foster were all due the same day."

"Whom does it leave me with?"

"Oddly enough, Patterson. You wouldn't think such a quiet little thing would buck the tide."

"You've never heard her in the PTA meetings, have you? A strong libber, God bless her."

Perry Dickson insisted we grace his church Sunday—that was his phrase. The ushers greeted us effusively, but some of their smiles were strained. Perry preached one of his most inspired, and shortest, sermons on prejudgment, prejudice and persecution. That his words were taken to heart was noticeable by the numbers of our acquaintances who came up to speak to the Kelloggs, Esther and me. I heard that Father Ryan took the same chapter and verse for his sermon. I promised that I would get to know that good man better in the very near future. If, after the exogenetic bit, he was still willing to speak to me.

The "slander" had fractionated people into those who were willing to believe incest, those who thought Peter and Cecily were adopting Pat's indiscretions, and those who were for or against unwed mothers, for or against abortion, for or against women's right to have complete say in what they chose to do with their own bodies.

"By God," Chuck said, for he insisted on coming up every Friday night, though it meant a mad streak down the Throughway on Monday mornings for his first appointments, "you've wiped drugs, moon-shots, the Middle East, not to mention elections, right out of conversations. And most of my colleagues tell me exogenesis is impossible."

We all greeted the day of the hearing with more relief than anxiety; such is the power of the easy conscience.

Since this was a hearing involving minors, it had to be held *in camera*. I would have preferred a public coverage so that when we were exonerated, as many people as possible would know. Because of the number of principals involved, we were assigned to one of the larger chambers. Unusual for such hearings, there were police officers, a bailiff, and a court secretary. Louise Baxter was conspicuous by her absence, which was as welcome to us as it was puzzling. Nor had all Jasper's probings elicited the name of the original complainant.

Judge Robert Forsyth was presiding, and he entered the chamber scowling—not a good sign, but he hated anything that smacked of the sensational, particularly when it involved children. He was, however, extremely perceptive and commonsensical.

"Oyez, oyez," rang the bailiff's cry as we got to our feet at Judge Forsyth's entrance. The rest of the initial proceedings were spewed out in a bored mumble. I noticed, cringing a bit, that when he cited the charge of "incestuous fornication and adultery," his enunciation promptly clarified and his delivery was strong.

"Yes, yes," said Judge Forsyth, waving him aside. "How do you plead?" he demanded of Pat and Peter.

"Not guilty, Your Honor," they said quietly.

"Is the presence of that animal in this courtroom necessary?" he asked, testily pointing to Wizard, who was sitting by Peter's side.

"Yes, Your Honor," said Jasper, rising. "Wizard is Mr. Kellogg's guide dog."

"Oh, indeed." It was obvious that Peter's deficiency had not been mentioned, nor had he heard the sly jibe circulating in town that Wizard had escorted Peter to the wrong bed one night.

The county prosecutor, Emmett Hasbrough, was an average-looking man with an above-average reputation for courtroom fireworks and results. His prefacing remarks were few, as he merely stated that he could easily prove that the charges were true and would like to proceed by calling the first witness. The judge waved assent and settled back in his chair, apparently far more engrossed in the water damage on the ceiling.

The delivery room nurse, looking both frightened and important, took the stand and gave the oath, her name, her occupation, and her current place of employment.

"On the morning of August 15, 1976, at 8:02 A.M., did you assist at the birth of twin girls?"

She nodded.

"To whom were these children born? Will you identify the mother if she is in the courtroom?"

"She is. She's sitting right there," said the nurse, pointing to Patricia.

"Now, is the father of the children in the courtroom?" Hasbrough glanced sideways at Jasper as if he expected an objection.

"Yes," said the nurse, and pointed at Peter.

"How do you know he is the father of the children?"

"I was still in the nursery where I had taken the children after their birth when he, and the other woman there, came to see them. He said he was their father."

"Thank you."

Smiling broadly, Hasbrough excused her and asked the admissions clerk of the hospital to take the stand.

"Were you on the admissions desk the morning of August 15, 1976, at the Mount Pleasant Hospital?"

"Yes, sir."

"Did you admit as maternity patient any woman seated in this court?"

Pat was duly pointed out.

"By what name was she admitted?"

"As Mrs. Cecily Kellogg."

Hasbrough shrugged as if to underscore his point and gestured toward Jasper that the clerk was his to cross-examine. Jasper rose, his pose thoughtful.

"Sir, I don't believe that you have reported that incident truthfully."

"Huh?" The clerk, clearly startled, glanced toward the prosecutor. Hasbrough shrugged again.

"Did this woman answer the questions herself?"

"Oh, well, no. Not actually. Uh, she was in labor, you see . . ."

"Come to think of it"—the clerk was embarrassed—"Mr. Kellogg did all the talking."

"Think carefully, now. When you asked him the patient's name, what precisely was his answer?"

The clerk thought a moment, confused. "But she's *listed* as Cecily Kellogg."

The judge advised him to answer the question to the best of his ability.

"It was some time ago . . ." Then his face brightened. "Yea. He said, 'My wife's name is Cecily Kellogg,' but I thought he meant *her!*" And again the man pointed to Pat.

"So Mr. Kellogg did not actually say that the woman he brought to you was Cecily Kellogg? Nor did she?"

"Well, no, put like that, I guess he didn't. But who else would I expect it to be?"

Jasper was finished making that point. Other members of the hospital staff were called, all substantiating the fact that Pat had been delivered of twins, and that Peter had openly admitted to being the father of the twins.

"That, Your Honor, is the case for the prosecution," said Hasbrough, not particularly bothered by the clerk's recital.

Judge Forsyth sighed, pursed his lips, and then turned inquiringly to Jasper. Beside me Cecily had torn the border from her handkerchief and was knotting it so tightly around her index finger that it was nearly cutting off the circulation. I carefully released it, and she smiled wanly at me.

"Your Honor, I move for a directed verdict," Jasper said, and Hasbrough gave a start of amazement.

"On what grounds, counselor?" demanded the judge, frowning.

"On the grounds that no incestuous fornication or adultery has yet been proved by the prosecution," replied Jasper, all innocence at the judge's reaction.

Judge Forsyth leaned toward him. "You have heard the testimony of several witnesses that Patricia Kellogg was delivered of two children whose paternity her brother, Peter, has not denied—in fact, has openly and unashamedly admitted. And you have the unutterable gall to tell me that no incest or adultery took place? I'm all ears, counselor," he said.

"I claim, Your Honor, that no incestuous fornication has been proved by these statements. The witnesses have confirmed that Patricia Kellogg gave birth to twins, the father of whom is Peter Kellogg. No one has proved that Peter Kellogg fornicated and committed adultery with his sister."

"If you can give me another logical explanation that satisfies my credulity, I wish you'd proceed. However, I will point out that consanguinity is also a felony in this state," and while the judge leaned back he was challenging Jasper to prove there was no inbreeding.

"Very well, Your Honor. I will now prove, irrevocably, that there was no act of fornication or adultery, nor are they guilty of producing children within the criminal degrees of consanguinity."

"Proceed, by all means," said the judge, steepling his fingers.

Jasper called Patricia to the stand. She took the oath with quiet dignity.

"Were you delivered of twin children on the morning of August 15, Miss Kellogg?"

"I was," Pat answered bravely and unashamedly.

"Who was the father of these children?"

"Peter Kellogg." The quiet answer fell on the silent room.

"Who was the mother?"

"Cecily Kellogg."

There was an audible reaction of disbelief from the prosecution's side.

"You can, of course," the judge drawled slowly, "substantiate that second statement?"

Jasper went on. "These are the separately kept records of Drs. Allison Seymour Craft, obstetrician of this town, and Charles Irving Henderson, consultant obstetrician of New York City. They have all been time-stamped, you will notice, on the hospital's time clock."

The judge made a moue of appreciation for that point and gestured for them to be brought to him. He leafed through several pages in each, frowning at the clinical details.

"The initial chapter," Jasper said, "in both accounts describes the process of exogenesis by which this birth was made possible. The actual propagation took place in the hospital operating room with both women under anesthesia and the father of the children in an anteroom, scarcely in a position to commit fornication and adultery with his sister. Even with the help of a guide dog."

"I beg your pardon, Mr. Johnson," the judge admonished him sternly, closing the record books with some force.

"Your Honor, I must object to the way this court's patience is being tried by the inclusion of these alleged records as proof of the innocence of the defendants. It's a preposterous alibi for an incredibly obscene act," said Emmett Hasbrough, on his feet with indignation.

"I shall admit the evidence. However, Mr. Johnson, I'm afraid this court is by no means convinced."

"I'll proceed with further evidence, Your Honor. Will Dr. Samuel Parker take the stand?"

Jasper quickly established Dr. Parker as the serologist of the University Medical School Hospital, thoroughly qualified to testify on his specialty. Dr. Parker admitted taking blood samples from Patricia, Cecily and Peter Kellogg, as well as from twin girls, four days old, whose footprints corresponded with those taken at the births of the Kellogg children. Dr. Parker admitted that he had been asked by Mr. Johnson to type these blood samples.

"Will you please tell the court the results of your tests?"

"Briefly, the man, Peter Kellogg, is a Type B negative, with a Pe factor. Cecily Kellogg is a Type B positive with a C factor, and Patricia Kellogg is a Type O negative with a Pa factor."

"You make a point of the difference in the additional factors?" asked the judge.

"Yes, I do, sir. We are able to type blood in more detail now than just A, AB, B and O. These additional 'factors,' as we call them, are every bit as important as the different types."

"I see. And what type were the children you examined?" asked Jasper.

"Both of them were Type B positive."

"Well, then, from her blood type, could *Miss* Kellogg possibly be the mother of the two children she delivered?" asked Jasper.

"I'm afraid to say it—but she *couldn't* be their mother," answered the serologist, puzzled by his own conclusion.

"Do you mean to tell me that the children *could* be *Mrs.* Kellogg's?" asked the judge, sitting bolt upright.

"I couldn't swear to that," the man admitted. "But I do most emphatically know that Miss Kellogg, that one, the defendant, could *not* be the mother of those children in spite of what I've heard today."

"How do you arrive at that conclusion?"

"Without getting too technical, although there are several substantiating factors besides the prime one, all children of a C and Pe blood factor *must* be Rh positive or heterozygous. All children of Pa and Pe factors *must* be Rh negative, which is homozygous, a recessive trait. So that Miss Kellogg, who is Pa, could not have had children with a positive Rh factor from Mr. Kellogg, who is Pe. So, while the blood types don't prove that *Mrs.* Kellogg is the mother from a serological standpoint, they prove that it is absolutely impossible for the babies' mother to have been *Miss* Kellogg. But that, of course, is itself impossible."

"Is there any chance the blood types were mixed, or that the infants differed from those in question?" asked the judge.

Instead of taking offense, Dr. Parker sighed.

"No, Your Honor. I checked my findings thoroughly—the children's footprints, everything involved. I had my assistant and one of the lab technicians check my findings and run two more complete serologies. Our results were identical."

"You may retire."

"Your Honor," said Jasper in the silence that ensued while
the bench pondered the evidence, "I admit that the scientific
proof is perhaps indigestible to the court. I would like to present one final piece of incontrovertible, and easily accepted,
proof." Judge Forsyth gave a curt wave of his hand to indicate
permission. "Bailiff, will you call Mrs. Louise Baxter to the
stand?"

Cecily gasped and clutched at me. I could only stare at the
unperturbed Jasper. None of us had had any notion that he'd
call her as a witness for us.

Louise Baxter walked down the center aisle, staring straight
in front of us, two angry spots of red on her cheeks, her mouth
firmly closed, her eyes flashing with suppressed emotion, and
every inch of her trim, elegantly attired body protesting the in-
dignity. When she took the stand, she refused to look at anyone. Her voice when she gave the oath and her name trembled
with anger and was so low the judge asked her to repeat her
name.

"You have one child, Mrs. Baxter, a daughter named
Cecily Baxter Kellogg, is that correct?"

Her lips pursed firmly as if she were about to repudiate
Cecily.

"Answer the counselor, if you please, Mrs. Baxter," said the
judge.

"Yes!" One tight word, and she spat it.

"Bailiff, please direct the attendants to bring in the persons
of Carla and Anne Kellogg."

Cecily half-rose as a nun (and I now remembered Dr. Dickson's enigmatic reference to the church's help) and the woman
warden brought in the babies. Jasper had got around Dr.
Dickson's kidnapping by saying that the parents, when they realized what a furor was being caused, had arranged for the

girls to be placed in an institution, where they were being anonymously cared for by qualified people. This was the first time Cecily had seen her children in almost three weeks, and she was perilously close to a complete emotional breakdown.

"Easy," I told her, putting my arm about her. "It's only a few moments more."

As the attendants reached the front of the chamber, Wizard rose and placed himself between the babies and Mrs. Baxter. I hadn't seen a hand signal from Peter. Fortunately, the judge was too preoccupied to notice the dog's insubordination.

"Your Honor," said Jasper, "it has been said by wise men that all the scientific proof in the world on paper is not worth one second's visual proof. Will you and Mr. Hasbrough please take a careful look at the two infants, and then at Mrs. Baxter?"

The judge peered over the high bench at the babies who were held up toward him. They were just beginning to rouse from sleep. He glanced at Mrs. Baxter, sitting rigid on the witness stand. He looked quickly back at the twins, muttering something inaudible to me, although the startled bailiff and Hasbrough both stepped closer to the babies. I craned my neck to try to see what they could be looking at.

"Oh, what is it?" breathed Cecily. "Why did Jasper bring Mother here?"

"Your Honor, I renew my motion for a directed verdict," said Jasper, with none of the inner satisfaction he must have been feeling.

The judge leaned back, staring with considerable respect at Jasper's tall, lean figure.

"You have made your point, counselor, and your motion is granted. As a matter of law, I hold that the evidence adduced by the defense is admirably sufficient to dismiss any hint of incestuous fornication or adultery, or consanguinity, that may have arisen from the evidence produced by the prosecution. Therefore, there is in fact no issue for determination. The defendants are not guilty as charged!"

He banged his gavel, Wizard barked twice, and we were all on our feet, yelling and crying, and I wasn't the only one weeping for joy.

Cecily scrambled to the babies. She all but grabbed Carla from the nun's arms and then turned with astonishment toward her mother. By that time, Chuck, Esther, and I were beside her. And we all saw what the judge had seen.

Dr. Dickson's mutterings hadn't registered with me on that frantic day, and I realized now that he had immediately seen that the twins were the spit and image of their maternal grandmother. From eyebrow tilt to the slight cleft in their little chins, they were miniatures of Louise Baxter. All the scientific documentation in the world was unnecessary in the face (I should say, faces) of such a strong familial resemblance. What a trick of fate!

Cecily suddenly moved forward toward her mother, sitting motionless on the stand.

"Look well, Mrs. Baxter," she said in a low voice, rich with the accumulated bitterness and uncertainty of the past weeks. "So help me God, it is the only time you will ever look on your granddaughters."

The only indication Mrs. Baxter gave that she had heard her daughter was to turn her head away.

Pat took Anne from the arms of the warden, and it was a measure of her acquitted innocence that she received a warm smile from the woman. The nun was assuring Cecily that the children had gained weight at a most satisfactory rate and she'd be glad to discuss their "vacation," as she sweetly put it, with Cecily at any time.

Chuck gave up pounding Jasper on the back and started

shooing us all toward the door. "Back home where we belong," he said.

No one had left the courtroom, so I don't know how word had reached the reporters, but when the officer at the door opened it, the hall outside was crowded, and the flashbulbs and the noise woke the startled babies.

"Miss Kellogg, will you do this again—for your brother and his wife?"

"Will you be a proxy mother for other deserving childless women?"

"Mr. Kellogg, how do you feel about . . ."

Jasper pushed his way to the front as Chuck protectingly put himself between Pat and the surging crowd.

"Now, now, boys," Jasper said, loudly but amiably. "We got some small girls here who need to get fed. Just let us through."

He and Chuck bowled their way past while Esther and I rear-guarded Cecily and Pat, my arm linked into Peter's.

"Please, now, this has been a trying experience for my clients. Later, fellas, later."

"Aw, come on, Mr. Johnson!" Several of the more aggressive were keeping pace with us, the others swarming in behind.

We were only to the cross-corridors when someone stepped on Wizard's paw, and he let out a hurt yipe, effectively halting our getaway.

"Esther, you take the babies to the car," said Pat, handing over Anne. "Let's get this over with, and they'll leave us alone."

"I didn't mean to step on the dog," the offender said earnestly, but he ruined the apology by getting a full-face shot of Pat in a very angry pose.

"Yes, let's," said Cecily, and handed Carla over to Esther, who hurried away, unhindered.

"No, I don't think my brother and sister-in-law would allow me to help them again," said Pat. "Once is enough. No, the next child I have will be my own. It's a lot easier socially to *be* the mother of the child you bear." She was grimly humorous.

"Do you think other women will consent to being host-mothers?"

"I wouldn't presume to say. But if people can be bought to take life, I expect there are some who can be paid to give life."

She was making a terrific impression on the reporters.

"How did you feel about having these babies?"

"It's not the most comfortable way to spend nine months," Pat said dryly.

"I mean," said the reporter insistently, "how *you* feel? Psychologically."

"My psychological reactions are my own."

"Oh, c'mon, Miss Kellogg, be a sport. There are millions of people waiting for the personal story behind this exogenesis."

"You forget," she reminded the reporter acidly, her eyebrows raising, "I have been a sport"—one of the group laughed at her double entendre—"and the personal story is much too personal. The facts are all I'll give. My brother's wife couldn't carry a child to term. There was no reason to suppose I couldn't. There was only one way in which that end could be achieved. I did it—with the medical help of Dr. Craft and Dr. Henderson. That's all."

She turned purposefully away, but one of the women reporters grabbed her arm.

"Do you support Women's Lib?"

Pat let out a forbearing sigh. "My philosophy is also private," and she broke through the group and went down the corridor as fast as she could. We tried to follow, with some success, but we were still being bombarded with questions.

"Will you set up in practice as an exogenic specialist, Dr. Craft?"

"I haven't had time to think about it."

"Had any offers from clinics and laboratories?"

"No comment," Chuck said grimly, and pushed Cecily and me on, while Jasper helped Peter.

"Do you plan to have children by exogenesis, Dr. Craft?"

"She won't have to," said Chuck, gripping my arm firmly as he hurried Cecily and me down the steps to my station wagon.

That was as much of a proposal as I ever did get from Charles Irving Henderson, but later, in private, he made his intentions so abundantly clear that I finally realized that his faithfulness had been prompted by an attachment to me, not to Pat or the Kelloggs.

Wizard made an excellent rearguard. He turned, darted, and snapped, and everyone fell back so that we got into the car without further harassment. Then Wizard daintily jumped into the open back window, his tongue hanging on one side of his mouth in a canine laugh.

"Home, O noble Ali," Chuck said to me, settling his arm around my shoulders as I turned the ignition key.

As we pulled away from the curb, Pat took young Anne from Esther, at which point the baby let out a squall of protest.

"Good heavens," exclaimed Patricia Kellogg with mock pique, "is that gratitude to the woman who gave you birth?"

PSI
CLONE

Joan Hunter Holly

"You're really certain, now, Counselor Minor?" the Assistant World Mediator asked for the third time. "Earth's survival as a livable planet depends on your judgment."

"It always does," Minor answered simply. "But I've given you my decision. There won't be any hostilities this time. The Ambassador from Sector Three is sincere about wanting to negotiate, and I found willingness to compromise in the Ambassadors from One and Two."

The Assistant Mediator still fidgeted. He was new on his job and hadn't dealt directly with Minor before. "I trust you completely, of course. We all do. A man with your talents—" He finally voiced his worry. "It doesn't seem exactly safe to let so much rest on the mental powers of one man, even though he is a Total-PSI."

"I agree," Minor said, bobbing his head. He wished to be away. He was too busy to stop and pat uncertain hands. "But since I carry the full responsibility, you can rest easy, Mediator. I went through the full course of what I'm expected to do at these sessions, including a deep-probe of each Ambassador to examine his thoughts, emotions, and basic motives. I've given my opinion, and I can't do anything more. Besides, Mediator—no one wants war." That was a condescending statement, and Minor knew it, but maybe hearing it spoken would ease the man's tension.

Ellis, Minor's bodyguard-companion, caught Minor's quiet glance and stepped in to end the conversation. "Counselor Minor has to board his carrier now, sir, or he'll miss his next appointment. So, if you don't mind . . ."

"Of course! Of course." The Mediator deferred to Minor quickly, as everyone did. "Take our thanks with you, Counselor."

Minor didn't wait for anything more. He strode briskly away, Ellis in his wake. They went out of the building and passed briefly through sunlight, then were shrouded inside a chauffeured limousine that hurried them to the carrier-port and Minor's private machine. It was really all he had to call "home," since he spent so much time in it flashing around the world. Yet it was an empty home. He seldom set eyes on the crew. The few he could call by name were the young women who served his meals and the man who took his dictation. Even they stayed clear of the cabin unless summoned.

Only Ellis remained with him all the time. Helpful, "Normal" Ellis, who hadn't a trace of PSI ability in his head, but was supposed to act as a friend to the world's only Total-PSI man.

Minor plunked into his seat, and the mere action of sitting down reported the tiredness of his body. He didn't much care for this day and let his sigh show it. He had cared less and less for every day, recently. Usually he managed to bury the pricking thought that pushed up from the bottom of his mind and

made him dissatisfied, but for the last six months that particular thought had become a near obsession.

Ellis noticed the sigh and asked, "Hungry? Do you want me
to ring for a sandwich?"

"Not yet." Minor looked at the blond young man who was
the only constant in his life and made a good contrast to his
own dark hair and black eyes. "Food isn't the answer."

"To what? What's the question? Your face is all down-lines
lately, Counselor, and since it's my job to see that you keep on
an even keel, I—"

"That Mediator voiced the question perfectly. Is it safe to
let the fate of the planet rest on the PSI abilities of one man?"

"Are you running into some self-doubts?"

"When have I ever been free of them? And I'm tired of
being everybody's trouble-shooter. If they didn't have me,
maybe they'd stay out of squabbles in the first place. As I told
the Mediator—no one wants war. So why do they keep on creating dangerous situations?"

"I can't answer any of that. But your powers are fantastic,
and you have confidence in your judgment, so don't let one
nervous first-timer bother you."

Minor harrumphed. "Confidence in my judgment is easy. I
know those Ambassadors inside out, once I go to work on
them. What haunts me is that sometime they may have a
change of heart after I leave—after I'm through monitoring
them. Human beings aren't totally predictable. If I'm wrong
about even one of them—if I miss the hint that he might
change his mind—then what happens to the Earth?"

Ellis shuddered, as every human being shuddered over the
shared specter of war. It wasn't the killing or the destruction of
man-made objects that stalked them, but the actual death of
Earth itself. One hundred years ago the H-bomb had threat-

ened that, but the H-bomb was a grain of sand compared to the boulder of Ecology.

Humanity had finally made peace with the planet by rigidly restricting population, then dispersing the giant cities into smaller centers that left "wild-space" between them, and mastering the use of clean solar power. The controls had restored the environment and the rule-of-the-natural. As a result, Life had more of its original meaning and value. But the balance was so carefully measured that warfare, with its debris, rotting flesh, and general disruption, could topple the environment off its foundation and crash the Earth down barren.

"Nothing like that will ever happen." Ellis was reassuring himself more than he was trying to help Minor. "You have every PSI power that exists. All at your command." He shrugged apologetically. "I guess I count on you as much as everyone else does."

"Right. One man to balance the world. Got a problem with war? Earthquake? Espionage? A psychopath? Call Minor."

Ellis's blue eyes were topped by a frown. "You've never talked this way before. I didn't even know you harbored such thoughts."

"There are a lot of things I don't talk about. Things I don't dare say, and things I have no words to say." Minor was surprised to hear himself admitting any of this. A private man, he clutched his privacy as close now as he had when he was a frightened boy who thought of himself as a freak. He added quickly, "Pay me no attention, Ellis. I'm just in a mood."

"That's what the 'companion' part of my job is all about."

"Instant Friend, you mean?"

"It was put to me that way, yes. But after three years with you, it's not a thing I can turn off and on anymore."

"Then forget that I made the remark, will you?" Minor apologized. Ellis *was* his friend—the only one he had.

"It's forgotten. But not the cause behind it. Be frank with me, Counselor. Is it good for you to brood? Can it interfere with your functions? Now you'll have to excuse that question, but I'm bound to ask it."

Minor chose to go along for a change. Ellis was willing to listen, and it would be a relief to open himself to the light, even if the greatest part of his soul had to remain hidden, as it always had. "Nothing can interfere with my PSI functions. I only wish to God something could! Maybe then I'd be more than a walking lie-detector seismographic oddity."

"Rarity, Counselor. You describe yourself like some kind of—"

"Freak," Minor said flatly. "That's exactly what I am and always have been. I've known it since I was nine years old. I knew it all through my adolescence, while I wore myself thin trying to hide what I was from the rest of the world."

"You didn't want to be known?"

"No freak wants to expose his freakishness. I'd still be hiding today if I hadn't hit into insanity when I was eighteen. I fell down right in the street—and then, of course, they had me. The doctors discovered what I was and told the authorities. Stams was assigned as Chief Psychiatrist and guardian, and that was that. I'm surprised you weren't briefed about the insanity. They didn't play fair with you."

"The way I was told, you suffered a nervous collapse from tension and exhaustion. Not insanity," Ellis said firmly.

"I was mollified with the same thing at the time. But Stams hints at the word 'insanity' once in a while. He always has."

"And you accept it because of your old ideas about yourself."

"Not at all. I accept it because it's logical. Wouldn't a mind like mine be more prone to insanity than a Normal's would be?"

"No." Ellis was adamant. "And if you want my opinion, Stams is more than a little afraid of you."

"The way he acts? He jerks me around like a puppy on a leash."

"That's his defense mechanism." Ellis kept on with his analyzing. "He brazens down his fear by subjugating you. By making you doubt yourself, he thinks he can control you. So far, it's worked. If you'd ever probed him, you'd know it for yourself."

"That's a nice idea, but I can't buy it." Minor glanced up quickly. "If it's true, then how do you suppress your fear of me?"

Ellis shrugged. "Easily. I'm simply not afraid of you, Counselor. Awed and sometimes mystified, yes, but not afraid. Some of the mystification comes right out of this conversation. Why did you ever want to hide yourself away? PSI power is an accepted thing. It's human progression. There are thousands of Telepaths. Surely you linked up with some of them and saw that you weren't a freak." He turned his head away. "I don't even like to say the word."

"I tried to join with them, but I always had to draw back. Can't you see, Ellis? I'm not a Telepath! I never was. What Telepaths can do, I can do five hundred times better. Plus so many things they've never dreamed of doing. I was as much a misfit with them as I was with Normals, and I lived scared to death that someone would find me out. No. I'm alone in the world. One of a kind."

"But you have full acceptance and a place of honor now. You're valued for your PSI power."

"I earn my place in society with it, and I don't mind the work or the responsibility, but I get tired. And I'm still lonely." He covered that last word quickly with others, because it laid bare too much of himself. "I'll tell you something else you

don't know. The earthquake forecast I did this week? The one
that took me forty minutes? It actually only took five. I stole
the other thirty-five minutes for myself. I stood there on that
open ground with my feet in the grass and the wind on my
skin and enjoyed the sensation of freedom. It made me late for
my appointment on the Sector Three espionage case, but I
stole those minutes, anyway. I always do. You'll leave me that
secret, won't you? You won't report to Dr. Stams that I'm pil-
fering time from his schedule?"

"I wouldn't think of reporting it. I enjoy the minutes in the
open myself. Earthquake forecasts are few and far between,
anyway."

"So they are."

They came only when seismologists with their cyclical-
graphs and measuring instruments decided a quake was im-
minent in some area. Then Minor was called. He stood in
the open, tuned himself to the Earth's magnetic fields, and,
through his long experience, gave a judgment of the severity of
the forthcoming quake, which in turn set in motion one of two
things: evacuation of nearby cities, or a show of confidence in
the quake-resistant strength of the cities' structures.

"But I'm heartened at even *that* breach of ethics in you,"
Ellis admitted. "You're so careful to stick to your own set
rules about using PSI power only with consent that I'm
amazed you'd do anything that wasn't common knowledge."

Minor smiled at him. Ellis had always chided him for being
too strict with himself. "Those rules are only decency. How
would you react if you felt I was inside your mind right now,
listening to your private thoughts, feeling your emotions second-hand, searching out your reasons for being friendly?"

Ellis looked at the floor, answering honestly, "I wouldn't
like it. I'd feel naked."

"Right. The only reason you can bear to be near me is that

you're sure I won't touch you without your consent. I may stand alone as some sort of valued misfit, but I'm not a monster." Minor leaned his head back, realizing how much he had confessed in the last minutes, and sorry he had done it. "Now we'll change the subject. Thanks for listening, but write it off as a momentary fit of self-pity."

"And let you go back into your shell and be your usual social recluse?" Ellis asked.

"You certainly come up with strange word images."

"Don't try to turn me off. If I'm your friend, then I'm your friend, and I got stuck on a certain word back there someplace. 'Lonely.' The way I see it, you're suffering from two things right now. You're tired from overwork, and lonely from being the only one of your kind. Am I right?"

"You are. But what does it matter?"

"A lot, because I have the solution to both problems, and Stams can just shove his orders to keep quiet. I'm going to give you the news now. If I have to, I'll tell him I couldn't hold out on *you,* anyway. That you took it right out of my mind."

Minor sat up straight, warning, "If this is something secret, then don't go any further. Protect yourself. Stams knows my standards. He'll never go for the idea that I picked your mind."

"Let him reprimand me if he wants to. I'm going to give you the news anyway. He doesn't have to take all of the satisfaction." Ellis clapped Minor on the shoulder. "Both of your problems will be over before you know it. Your workload will be shared, and you'll have a real friend. One who can function on your own mental level."

Minor stared at him, resisting the temptation to break into Ellis's mind and grab his entire meaning all in one instant.

A smile was waiting to burst across Ellis's face as he said, "Stams called me this morning while you were at the session. Your Clone is ready, Minor! Ready to meet you, learn from you, and share your life. How's that for a stimulant? Make you feel less lonely?"

Minor sat frozen. He couldn't answer quickly—not after all these years of waiting. The spark that had made its home in the bottom of his mind suddenly flared to a fire, since he didn't need to repress it anymore. All he could finally say was, "Does he have a name?"

"M-I-N for Minor, and C for Clone. Minc."

"And he's eighteen years old."

"I think you look pleased," Ellis said.

"I'm relishing. You don't know how much I— Minc! So that's what they called him." He was silent for a long moment. After eighteen years of waiting, he was at last going to inherit his own image. Another thought struck him. "Where are we headed, Ellis? I never asked. Have I been assigned to another piece of work?" It was ridiculous even to consider working now.

"You wouldn't do it if you had been. I can see it in your face. No, Counselor, we're heading straight for Minc."

"I can't stand much more of this!" Minor quit pacing the carpet in the dark-paneled office and stopped before Ellis, threatening, "I'm going to break loose and use PSI if they don't hurry. I'll meet him *mentally* if they won't let us come face to face."

"No, you won't," Ellis said gently, yet emphatically. "Dr. Stams expressly ordered you not to do that, and you don't go against his orders."

Minor eyed Ellis soberly, knowing too well that he was right and wishing he weren't. Stams had become obnoxiously possessive in the last few years, manipulating Minor and expecting Minor's compliance with everything he dictated. "So I won't," Minor agreed. "But what can be taking so long? Stams

can't offer me a thing like this and then torture me by making
me wait."

Ellis hid his surprise at Minor's unusual display of tempera-
ment under a shower of soothing words. "Why don't you sit
down and let me bring you some coffee? You're nerving yourself up to a high. Where's your patience? Minc has existed for
eighteen years, and you've managed to live with the fact that
you couldn't be together. What are a few minutes more?"

"Every one of those eighteen years was hell!" Minor's black
eyes locked on Ellis's blue ones, and his voice lowered to a
half-curse. "These minutes are agony."

"I understand."

"No, you don't. Thanks for trying, but you don't understand. When you're one of a kind, with no one to share your
reality—" He turned away, letting the admission come as it
would. "My Clone will share it. We'll truly 'know' each other
—the good things *and* the horrors that come with Total-PSI. I
won't be the one who has to understand everybody else anymore. For a change, I'll be understood."

Minor began pacing slowly, needing to explain his feelings
to someone, even if he still had only Ellis to hear them. "Ever
since they took that cell from me eighteen years ago, I've had
to fight against searching for him. I lost the fight more times
than I like to admit, and I sent out mental feelers during my
trips around the world. But I never caught a trace of him.
Stams kept me just far enough away from this location. He
knows my power range—how much distance my mind can
travel—and maneuvered me away from here.

"Now I'm standing on the spot, but I'm ordered not to
reach out for what is mine, and I'm even being kept from
going to him physically. How do you think I feel? I need that
boy, Ellis. My bones ache to have him. Another human being
like me! Not 'like' me, even; he is me. He'll be closer than a

son, closer than a brother, and he'll end the interminable loneliness." He halted, embarrassed. "Ignore me, will you? I think
the tension has set my tongue flapping."

"If that's the case, I'm glad for it. I've been of some real use
for a change, if only as a sounding board. I turned out to be
some great kind of friend, didn't I? I haven't known you at all.
Or helped you."

"You've been all you could possibly be, and I'm just wallowing in frustration at the moment. My main point is that just
as I'll finally have someone who can understand me, so will
Minc have someone. After eighteen years alone, he must be
desperate, too. I was, when I was his age. Minc needs me and
I need him, and Stams is pushing me too far this time."

"That's an impossibility," Stams's voice said from behind
him. "You're stronger than all the rest of us put together,
Counselor."

Minor whirled about, expecting to see Stams and Minc
standing there together, but Stams was alone, his figure too
familiar—short, round and graying.

Stams said in his habit of condescension, "A thing like this
takes time, Counselor. It has to be handled delicately. You'll
meet the boy soon enough, but first you have to hear from the
man who raised him."

"Why?" Minor demanded. "Put Minc and me together and
we'll know all about each other instantly. Total-PSI power
means that, Dr. Stams. If the cloning worked, and he is my
exact duplicate—" Minor spoke his haunting fear of eighteen
years.

"He is," Stams said. "He has every ability you have. He
lacks only your experience in using it. That's why, barring a
real world emergency, I'm allowing you an extended leave to
tutor him and bring him up to your level without waiting for
him to learn through trial-and-error."

"You're making us both sound like machinery, Stams," Minor complained, "and I've never appreciated—" He was cut off by the opening of the door.

Another man stepped into the office. He was short and youngish, with brown hair and a faint smile that betrayed a grudge when it fell on Minor. Allowing himself one instant of ethical lapse, Minor delved into him slightly and came up with his name—Bates, Ph.D., M.D. The grudging smile stemmed from Bates's unwillingness to turn over his coveted Clone to other hands.

With guilt nudging him for intruding on the doctor's mind uninvited, Minor shook Bates's hand and nodded his sticky way through the flattering words about being honored to meet the PSI Counselor of the world. He didn't want flattery. He knew who and what he was. Right now, he wanted only his Clone.

But he wouldn't demand to see him. He seldom demanded anything. He could easily have taken anything he wanted through his PSI powers, but he kept close restraints on himself and always had. "A character fault," Ellis forever told him, saying he clung so hard to his own sense of decency that it blocked him from being all he could be. Ellis was probably right, but Minor couldn't help it. He preferred to follow his own way.

Bates was saying, ". . . and so the boy has been raised carefully and in the best surroundings. He's been allowed to grow and experiment as he's seen fit. I've had an amazing eighteen years, watching over him. He's astounded me almost daily with the things he can do. He's even frightened me at times, if you'll excuse my saying so. And meeting you, Counselor Minor—the fully mature and experienced proto-type of Minc—well, a man can be forgiven some uneasiness, wouldn't you agree? Your powers are tested and tried. You're a real force to be—"

Minor blocked the words out again. Bates was afraid of him, but so was everyone else, at first. He supposed they never got over it entirely, no matter what he did to make them feel secure around him.

". . . and this is a momentous occasion," Bates was continuing when Minor tuned back in. "It doesn't happen often, you know."

"I'm aware of that," Minor told him, holding down his impatience.

"Cloning is seldom practiced with human beings. Since we want our population stable, it's illogical to duplicate people. Cloning is only allowed with food animals, the best of them. The best animals and the really unique men. Such as you."

"You don't have to pat my ego anymore, Dr. Bates," Minor said, becoming rude. "I believe you came to fill me in on Minc's background."

Bates went slightly pale at Minor's severe tone. "Yes, of course I did. I'll tell you how each power developed in him, and at what age, and—"

"Excuse me," Minor interrupted, "but, Dr. Bates, will you permit me to enter your brain and extract the information for myself? That way, I can have it in a few seconds, and we can proceed with our main purpose."

Bates shifted from one foot to the other and glanced apprehensively at Stams. With Stams's nod of assurance, Bates agreed to the probe. "But take only the information on Minc," he put in nervously.

Minor dove into the man's brain headfirst and found the data to be what he had expected. Paralleling his own development, Minc had shown his first signs of thought-reading at two

years; empathic emotion-and-motive sensing at three; teleki-
nesis at five; and—

Minor straightened sharply. Why should Bates's mind rattle
on with "hypnosis at eight" and "thought control at nine"?

But of course! Minor smiled to himself. The cloned boy had
discovered those side powers and tested them as Minor had,
but because Minc was so closely observed, he had been caught
at it before he put them aside of his own accord as too dangerous and unethical for use.

Minor spoke to Bates. "Thank you, Doctor. I have it all.
His childhood was a duplicate of mine, except that I thank-
fully didn't find any hint of his being in danger of a nervous
collapse such as the one I suffered at eighteen. That was due
entirely to my environment, then. I hoped that would be true.
He's been accepted from the beginning, while I spent those
years cringing." He cleared his throat. "I do have one question.
You were hesitant to let me into your mind, yet I clearly saw
that the boy probes you all the time, no? Am I right to think
you're still allowing him a free ride through the minds of your
staff?"

"Naturally! How can he be stopped?"

"Only by himself—and that means me. I'll be sure that one
of the first things I teach him is that an individual's mind is
sacrosanct unless consent is given to probe it. He'll learn
quickly."

"He always has." Bates smiled, back on familiar ground.
"He's a brilliant student."

"He'll learn even more quickly now, Doctor, because he'll
clutch concepts and the reasons behind them directly out of
my brain. I don't like the idea that he's using his PSI powers so
freely, but it won't be hard for him to understand why he has
to restrain them unless they're requested."

Stams put in, "Counselor Minor learned all of that harshly —out of fear of giving himself away. His Clone will be able to undergo those bad experiences second-hand. Less painfully, but just as decidedly. Right, Counselor?"

"Exactly. And, now?" Minor left it hanging. He was keeping himself from shouting at them only through force of will. Would they never take him to the boy? Simply by opening a door they could double the population of his world and give him a fellow being to "speak" with in fire-quick telepathy, "feel" with in quivering empathy, "exist" with, at last, contentedly. "Is he ready for me?"

Minor approached the door alone. It was painted a pale green, a color of calm, but he was churning. He was nearing the biggest, happiest moment of his life and didn't know what he should say when he met it. Should he go in wide open? Or hold back and allow Minc the first move?

He turned the doorknob, took two firm steps across the threshold, and heard the door click shut behind him. He was in a twelve-by-fourteen blue-carpeted room, furnished with a sofa and upholstered chairs, a bookcase wall, and gentle light. He saw it all as a side-blur, because there was a figure waiting there, and it was turning to face him.

When the other eyes came around, Minor clutched the back of the nearest chair, stunned out of sense for a moment.

There he was! *He—HIMSELF* of the past—wearing a face that didn't look back from his own mirror anymore because eighteen years had intervened with their lines and changes. The renewed sight of that face brought sudden shock as the emotions of being eighteen crashed in on him all at the same time, reflection and memory together.

"Minc?" he asked, sorry to hear his voice so hesitant when

he had envisioned this as a rushing for each other—a shouting, a joy. "You're Minc." Of course there was no question of it.

"And you're Counselor Minor," the boy answered.

Minor strode across the room, wanting to embrace the boy, but Minc only thrust his hand forward, and the meeting became a handshake. The boy ended it quickly, and Minor stood like a ship with no anchor. But he was wide open, his barriers unintentionally down, and he caught Minc's thoughts of, *"So this is how I'll look when I'm forty. Not a bad prospect—except for the eyes."*

Minor smiled. The boy was seeing him as an older, upcoming version of himself. Minc had no memory of being forty, while Minor recognized every jut and curve of the younger face. It had once been his own.

"What's wrong with my eyes?" Minor responded telepathically.

"They have ghosts in them," Minc answered just as silently.

"But yours flash with black sparks. I'm glad of that."

Minc appeared startled and stepped back. *"He's hearing my thoughts! No one can do that to me—I wondered how it would feel—it doesn't."*

"You didn't know that?" Minor let his surprise radiate full force as he brought the PSI conversation back to the personal basis of "you" and "I," instead of "he." *"You've never spoken through PSI?"* Hadn't Bates supplied this boy with a Telepath-companion? For practice, at least?

"Bates never supplies me with anything!" Minc answered the unvoiced question harshly. *"Only ooh's and aah's over what I can do. But you're listening to my mind!"*

"Naturally. It's my normal medium."

"Would you please stop? I think I'm afraid of it."

Minor was bewildered, but he immediately put down his

barriers against the boy's thoughts and said, full-voice, "There's nothing to fear, but we'll speak aloud if you like. Maybe you need time to get used to two-way PSI."

"That's probably it, so please don't use it for now." Minc answered in Minor's own, younger voice. Then he stepped away, shielding his face as he said, "You wanted to do it *all* through PSI, didn't you? You wanted us to melt together, or something."

"Only to get acquainted. It won't hurt to handle it this way until you're more relaxed. I expected you to be anxious to jump into the PSI world and have your first full experience."

"I am. But later on, maybe." Minc faced him again. "Don't misunderstand or be disappointed. I do want to know you."

"Quit worrying about me. I've come to learn about you, and how your life has been."

"You already know that. We're the same, so our lives are the same."

"Not a bit. You've grown up aware that what you are is acceptable, while I grew up thinking I was a misfit."

Minc's black brows came together over his blacker eyes. "Why would you ever think that? It's the other people who are the misfits. They're zeros! Adoring zeros. They think we're some kind of gods."

Minor smiled at him, sure that he, Minor, understood, but wishing he could delve into the boy's emotions to be certain. "Protest all you like, but I know from experience what goes through a boy's head when he sees that he's different from everyone else. Of course, you knew that I existed. That may have eased some of it."

"Certainly! It's wonderful to grow up knowing you're not really yourself, but just a copy of someone else. That you're a no-person with a no-name— M-I-N for Minor and C for Clone. What are you supposed to be to me, anyway? My father?"

Minor had never considered the point, and he stumbled on it. "Well, no, I don't suppose—"

"'No' is right. A parent-cell, maybe, but never a father."

Minor absorbed the sharp words without responding. The boy was resentful and needed his understanding. He said gently, "I'll never pretend to be your father, then. But I am a strong man, Minc. Someone you can lean on. And I'm offering myself for that."

Minc's flare of resentment vanished, and he spoke more gently, too. "Would you believe that for a while I was stupid enough to search for you? Mentally? But I never caught a trace of your mind, and after a time I quit trying. Then it was easy not to believe any of Bates's story. Until today."

"I see. I'm a shock to you. I didn't expect to be." Minor found himself edging forward and stopped. He wanted to touch the boy, to let his physical grasp say what Minc had forced him to keep his mind from saying. "The last thing I want is to make you unhappy."

"Obviously." Minc was sharp again. "I could suffocate in the emotions you're oozing. You came in here as though you were rushing to some new world, and now you're ready to dissolve into a lump of pity. You're more transparent than anybody I've ever met, and I don't much like it."

"I'm transparent to you because we're the same person. I admit that I came in here wanting something special to happen. It hasn't. And it can't, until you allow it. Minc, let's take down the barriers and open ourselves wide. Let's learn each other once and for all. It will be so much easier than this. So much better."

"No!" Minc backed away. "You leave me alone."

"You're afraid of me?" Minor couldn't believe it.

"Stop reading my emotions!" the boy challenged. "Get out of me. You're deep enough in me already—cell for cell. I don't ever want to go down inside *you*. You're too powerful. I can feel it."

Minor stood nonplused. There were finally two people in his world, but one was afraid of the other. He had to stop being a scapegoat for this boy and take the situation in hand. "If you're sensing my emotions, then you're not abiding by your own bargain. You asked me not to touch you on a PSI level, but you're draining the insides out of me. I've been standing here naked to you, haven't I?"

"You always will. I'm powerful, too!"

Minc's threat was desperate bravado, and Minor backed down. He was frightening the boy. He'd invaded Minc's life as a half-believed-in, half-feared power figure, expecting to fulfill his own dreams. It had all gone wrong, and the hurt was a thing he couldn't hide. Worse, Minc was fully aware of it. The boy could read him like glass, and was doing so.

"I'm sorry I put you in a corner, Minc. I shouldn't have been critical. You've handled your life in the best way you could, just as I did. But don't be afraid of me. I won't intrude on your mind without your consent. I didn't come here to hurt you, for God's sake!"

"You came to absorb me. To really make me you."

"That's a ridiculous idea. I only want your PSI companionship, someone I can actually talk to, feel with, a chance to make use of my own ability for something besides a monitoring device."

"It adds up to the same thing."

"It doesn't!" Minor held strong rein on his patience. "We're different enough because of our backgrounds to always remain different. You can't stand there and tell me you haven't been lonely, because I'll never believe it. The first mutation of anything has to be lonely."

"I'm not the first."

"No. I am. But you may as well have been, since we've been kept apart." Minor stepped forward again, aching to explain. "Look, Minc—there are things and places in my mind I've never explored because I haven't had a matching mind to help me. There are emotions I can't express verbally or even tele- pathically. But because I have them, I need to express them. You can experience them as I do—at the same moment—and really comprehend what I'm feeling. I can do the same for you."

"What makes you so sure I want it?"

"Because we're the only two of us in the world, boy. It's the same as though one man in the primitive past had been handed a fluent language, full-blown, so he could express his ideas, but no one else could understand the sounds he made. He would have been left screaming at the sky. I've felt like that."

Surprisingly, Minc said, "The way you talk is embarrassing. You show all of yourself with words. You don't even need PSI."

"You're telling me to be ashamed for speaking honestly. I'm not. And what I've told you, I've never told anyone else. As far as the rest of the world is concerned, these things don't even exist in me. But you must have discovered by now that hypersensitivity is one of the worst riders on our PSI power. We feel more deeply. I've come to the conclusion that we even feel in different *ways* than Normals do. Since I can't find any words to communicate so many of my emotions, it must be that Normals haven't felt the same emotions. If they had, they would have invented language symbols to describe them."

Minc stared at him blankly, and Minor couldn't read what might be going on behind the sharp black eyes. On this non-PSI level, the boy was shut away from him.

Minor shook his head in frustration. "You don't understand

what I'm saying, do you? If you'd only open up and let me—
We have so much to learn about each other— Ourself—but
you're not letting it begin! I need to be taught, too, you know,
and you're the only one in the world who can do it. We have
to study together, explore, grow."

"Sure," Minc scoffed. "You're going to teach me how to
forecast the strength of earthquakes, or touch a piece of evidence and know who committed a crime, or be a lie-detector.
Plus, how to make myself subservient and turn on and off at
somebody else's command."

"You make it sound unclean. It's not. I'm my own man.
We'll merely earn our keep with those things—not that they
aren't important to the world, because they are. You're being
deliberately stubborn or you'd understand what I'm saying.
Our life is what we have to explore. And live." He was pleading, but he didn't care. "Believe me, boy, being the only one of
your kind is not living!"

"And the turning on and off at somebody's orders?"

"Is only decency. You're afraid of me in spite of the fact
that you're just like me. How do you think a Normal reacts
when he thinks I'm monitoring every thought and emotion he's
sending out? Once you and I are tuned to each other, you can
learn what I have to teach you about our work in a few days.
We'll spend years exploring Ourself."

"But first I have to lay myself wide open to you, right?"

"Exactly. What's so difficult about that?"

Minc's doubts were clear on his face. "I'm just not ready.
These things are all your goals, and I have plans of my own. I
haven't hibernated here, you know. My plans are—" He
stopped abruptly. "No. I can't tell you. I don't know you well
enough to trust you that far."

"You never will until you do trust me for the few necessary
minutes of the first merging. But I'll tell you one thing. We

can't fail. We're expected to work together, and we can't fail to do it. We can't throw the years away—the ones you've spent growing and being so expensively protected, and the ones I've been damned to live alone since I was born."

Minc's eyes were black steel. "You certainly come on hard, Minor. You're angry and bitter, too, aren't you? Well, you can relax a little about our work. I intend to cooperate with you. As for the rest . . . I have to get accustomed to you and find out what kind of man you are."

Minor sighed softly, sensing a small victory in this unexpected game of hostility. "That can be done in no time, if you'll simply give the word."

"Not yet." Minc held up his hand, as though shielding himself from a physical threat. "Soon, maybe, but not yet. Let me keep the little individuality I have for a while longer. And let me weigh your character. Remember, Minor, you're asking a lot of me. Whatever it is that you are, I might have to become."

Even without the aid of PSI insight, Minor felt the boy's fear of losing his personality, of drowning and turning into someone unknown to himself. He realized instinctively that it was time to end this first meeting. His anticipated hopes hadn't materialized, but it was time to end it.

Minc, still monitoring him on a shallow level, caught his decision before he voiced it. "Is that all for now, then?"

"Since I'm just as confused as you are, yes. It hasn't been all I had planned, but then I've never met myself before."

Minor went to the door. As he reached for the knob, Minc said from behind him, almost wistfully, "Minor? I do want to be with you. I really do have plans and needs in my life, and I don't think I can manage them alone."

Minor swung back to look soberly at this young duplicate of himself. "I'll come back tomorrow, and we'll see how we get along then. It depends on your willingness, Minc. Just remember—I'm ready any time you are."

He opened the door and left the boy standing alone, wanting to smash down that image because it reminded him that he was still standing alone, too.

He walked slowly back to Bates's office on previous instructions to return and report. Still caught in the throes of determining his own emotions, he was reluctant to report anything. Was he more disappointed than angry? Or vice versa?

All he knew for certain was that the one moment in his life that was supposed to have been entirely his hadn't even happened.

He had learned to live with disappointment years ago, but this one was too personal. He couldn't let Stams or Bates know, not when they viewed him only as a valuable tool. Mostly, he couldn't let them know because they wouldn't care, and he wanted someone to care. So, to conceal his mixed feelings, he homed in on the anger. It might carry him through their questions.

All three men were in the office, Stams and Bates seated near the desk, and Ellis alone in an orange chair in the corner. Ellis almost jumped to his feet at Minor's entrance, his expression asking silently, "Was it all you wanted it to be? All you dreamed?"

Minor only grazed Ellis's expression with his glance, holding fast to his anger.

Stams spoke first. "How did it go? What's your estimation, Counselor?"

"Yes, what do you think of him?" Bates was eager.

"I think he's exactly what he is. My eighteen-year-old copy," Minor hedged.

"That's not an answer," Stams said. "We're already aware of that. What we're after is your judgment of the meeting."

"I don't want to talk about it yet. I'm not ready for discussions. My reactions are still too personal to be objective."

"That's one thing they definitely are not." Stams hammered in his authority. "You're duty bound to—"

"When I have something to report, I'll do it." Minor raised his voice to overpower Stams's. "Now that the boy is in my hands, I intend to handle the relationship in my own way and at my own speed."

"There's no time for dallying. What's more, you don't have the authority to do as you please. You're here solely to instruct Minc and to do it quickly. I've granted you an extended leave, not a vacation to use for your own purposes."

"I'll begin the instruction as soon as I can. First we need time to get acquainted."

"You said that would be instantaneous once the two of you were together," Stams pointed out.

"So I did. But he's more complex than I expected. Maybe because I'm more complex than I realized. Or you realized. I intend to take my time and keep things confidential while I do it."

"Minc is still in my charge," Bates protested, guarding his own territory. "I'll back Dr. Stams in forcing your reports if I have to."

"Force all you want, but you won't have reports until there's something worth reporting. On the other hand, try this for a starter, Bates. I disagree totally with the way you raised him. I wasn't allowed a voice in it, so naturally you blundered."

Bates defended himself. "I raised that boy perfectly. I saw to it that he has none of your character faults, which Dr. Stams carefully pointed out to me as overzealousness, insecurity, and a state of being conscience-ridden."

"Minc is one of the most insecure human beings I've ever

laid eyes on," Minor argued. "Are you aware that he thinks of himself as nothing more than a copy? As a nothing? You didn't teach him self-worth, and that was the main area where his life could have been different from mine. Instead, you made him grow up alone, just as I did." The blaming felt unreasonably good, burying the deflated dreams Minor had carried into the room.

"Minc has never pictured himself as a freakish misfit," Stams said, nastily underlining Minor's own feelings.

"No?" Minor let the word hang for a delicious moment. "The only difference between us is that he thinks he's an accepted freak. To bungle eighteen years, a fortune in expenditures, and a man's—"

"Enough!" Stams drew himself up to his full height, which could never bring his head level to Minor's, no matter how hard he tried. "The Clone was handled scientifically and will continue to be dealt with that way. Your role is to get him on a solid working basis, not to reshape his personality."

"Most definitely," Bates said, taking unusual courage from Stams's attack. "Just because he didn't quite perform as you wanted him to . . ."

Bates froze at the sudden turn of Minor's eyes, which caught him in mid-sentence. "Did you have a listening device in that room?" Minor demanded. He held his breath, waiting for the answer. If they had overheard the entire encounter, then they already knew of his failure and how he was trying to hide it. He would seem a fool.

Bates reacted nervously, as though he were impaled on the end of Minor's pointing finger. "No! I never considered it, Counselor. Believe me!"

"Then don't consider it," Minor ordered, and protected himself by adding, "That's one area of your mind I'm not going to keep my hands off. If you place an eavesdropper, I'll know it. If you press the boy for information, I'll know that, too. I'll figure out your consequences afterward."

With Bates shrinking from the threat, Minor strode out of the office, trailed by an astonished Ellis, who had never before seen a flare of temper in his PSI charge during all the years he'd been with him.

In their private suite—two bedrooms and a living area—Minor shut himself away from Ellis, thinking his own thoughts and even eating dinner alone. Finally, at ten o'clock, he wandered into the living room and found the yellow-haired man sitting there, holding a book but not reading it. He'd obviously been waiting out Minor's isolation.

"I'm sorry I kept to myself so long," Minor opened. "This is an empty place, and I should have been more company for you."

"I didn't expect you to be. Not after an experience like the one you had. It's not every day that a man meets his own Clone. Of course, it might happen often with you. Since this cloning proved a success, you can bet Stams will authorize more."

"I'll populate the world with myself." Minor attempted a smile.

Ellis looked down at his book. "Something went wrong, didn't it? It wasn't what you expected it to be."

"There wasn't any joy in it, if that's what you mean, Ellis. None at all. The boy is full of resentment against me. His attitude threw me, and I handled him awkwardly. We didn't touch minds."

"But that's impossible!"

"Not when you realize that he's afraid of me. He's everything I thought he'd be, with the sorry additions of fear, bitter-

ness, and this awful idea that because he's a Clone, he's nobody."

"I see. You feel sorry for him, and you're making excuses.
Well, I'm considering you. If he displayed all of those things,
it must have been a terrible experience for you. No wonder
you scared hell out of Bates that way."

"That was self-protection. I don't want anyone to overhear
my personal failure." Minor plopped down in a chair. "It isn't
actually failure, either. I've spent the afternoon trying to trade
places with Minc, and I believe I understand him now. He has
a case. Irrational, but still a case. He didn't really believe I
existed, so he made plans for himself, and then I appeared and
threatened to destroy them. He doesn't even own his name!
But I was right to guess he'd be lonely. He proved that when I
was leaving. He needs me, but he doesn't quite dare reach for
me. Anyway, it will work out if I give it time."

"More time!" Now Ellis was impatient. "Look, this is none
of my business, but I know how you were counting on that
meeting. What it meant to you. You've waited for eighteen
years, Minor! You shouldn't have to wait any longer. He
wouldn't let you into his mind?"

"Not one fraction."

"Then the entire experience was lost as far as you're concerned, and that makes me mad." Ellis's blue eyes fired in a
way Minor hadn't thought blue eyes could spark.

"You have it wrong. The experience simply hasn't happened yet. It will. Minc and I are bound too closely for anything else. My fault was in believing we'd have instant rapport.
That couldn't be."

"Why not? You're just alike."

"Not really. Our different backgrounds mean different
viewpoints and reactions. Don't be so concerned about it,
friend. Minc will come to me."

Ellis was silent, musing for a moment. "Will this . . . merging be painful to him?"

"Of course not. There's no sensation involved. It *will* be an emotional shock for him to take in my forty years of life all at once, especially the turmoil I felt when I was his age. Those experiences could overwhelm him, but I've considered that, and I'll be right there to guide him through. Since he'll also feel my strength, he himself will come out the other end stronger."

"And doing it will give you what you need?" Ellis questioned on, heading somewhere Minor couldn't imagine.

"Yes. Once done, we'll be one—locked together and never alone again."

Ellis stood up, his lithe body straight and determined. "Then, I say, don't let him get away with it! Throw him into the water and let him find out he can swim!"

Minor shook his head, smiling. "Thanks for standing on my side, but don't waste your anger. You know I won't rush him. That would destroy our relationship before it began. Besides . . ."

"You don't intrude without consent," Ellis finished for him. "This case is different, Minor. You said yourself that Minc wants you. It's your responsibility to show him what's waiting for the two of you."

"I will. But gently. Remember, he's only eighteen—probably younger, emotionally. Minc and I are waiting to see what tomorrow brings, so why don't you join me in a nightcap and add yourself to the side of patience?"

Ellis relaxed his body in one great gesture of futility. "When I decided to be your friend, I picked out a mountain of a job, didn't I? I'm beginning to think you're too much for any Normal to fathom. You live in another world."

In the morning, Minor sidestepped the officials and went

directly to his appointment with Minc, determined to let the
boy lash at him all he would and take it in stride while he
worked at convincing Minc to come home to his God-given
PSI life. He drew a deep breath before he entered, preparing
to face a wary tiger. But Minc surprised him. When the boy
saw Minor, his face brightened with eagerness.

"Good morning, Counselor! I'm glad you came back. I was
afraid you wouldn't, after the way I behaved yesterday."

"I don't frighten off that easily," Minor answered with relief. This might be the day. Minc's outward expression was
promising. "Although I admit to a restless night, while you
look as though you'd slept the sleep of angels."

"I did—after I talked with Dr. Stams. I hope you don't
mind, but I asked him about you, and I—"

"Took a bit more than verbal answers from him?" Minor
winked.

"I needed the rest to be sure," Minc confessed. "By doing it,
I found out that he knows you better than anybody else does,
and that he trusts you."

"He's ridden on my back since I was your age. Does his
good reference mean that you can trust me, too?" *Please let it
mean that,* Minor hoped.

"Are you monitoring my thoughts?" Minc abruptly changed
direction.

"Of course not."

"Then . . . yes, I can trust you." He held up his hand at
Minor's inner leap of excitement. "Don't jump to conclusions.
I only mean that I can trust you enough to talk openly. I still
don't want the PSI thing. I thought we'd stay on a vocal level
for one more meeting and compare notes about the—*our*—
powers. Nobody around here understands what it's like to
have them. We can get acquainted as though we're Normals
today, and then—who knows?"

"Vocal it is. A shoddy substitute, but acceptable. Who begins? I have a feeling it's supposed to be me."

"If you would. Please." Minc added the polite word like an awkward child.

Minor sat down and began to dig into his past, skimming over the dull spots. Minc sat down, too, and was soon interjecting comments as Minor unfolded the events in his discovery of his abilities. The story of his near fall into insanity at first fascinated the boy, then made him uneasy, so Minor quickly finished with that and returned to relating how he had learned to channel his powers into areas that were useful to the world.

He concluded, "I've come out with a good measure of respect and value, Minc. I have a definite place, and necessary work to do. If you'll grant me a little ego, I save lives *and* the planet."

"That's not ego. It's true. I'll be doing that, too?" The boy was alight, caught up in the sight of himself receiving deference and gratitude. "You've used the PSI as I figured you would. Isn't it glorious to have such control? I know that already, in my own limited way. You can make people think whatever you want them to think, and it's a sensation you can't describe to anyone who can't do it himself. Does it give you the same feeling of power it gives me? Or has the edge worn off for you?"

Minor was startled. "We're out of sync here. What you're describing is thought control, and I've never gone in for that. I leave it totally untouched. You're not saying *you* use it?"

"Naturally! I plant ideas in these zeros' heads all the time, and they think they thought them up. It's some of the best fun I have. You really don't?" He looked at Minor oddly. "Then what about hypnosis? We can hypnotize in an instant. How do

you feel when you're making people go around like mario-
nettes doing what you order?"

Through a sudden clutch of wariness, Minor made himself
remember that Minc had been encouraged to run at will
through the minds of the staff members, and said only, "I
don't go in for hypnosis, either. It's unethical."

Minc blinked in disbelief. Then he stood up, and his next
words were scornful. "And you're supposed to teach *me?* With
all the things you don't know about our power, *I* should be the
teacher. You haven't taken half of what you deserve for yourself. You've been just plain stupid."

"Ethical is the word, Minc. And decent. You'll have to
learn the meaning of those two qualities. That will come easily
when—"

"Oh, no, Minor. *You'll* have to learn the meaning of what it
really is to be Us. And you will. From me! When we work together on my plan, we'll have to cooperate all the way."

Minor's stomach was a mass of icicles. Something in what
the boy was saying wasn't right, and was leading to a place he
didn't want to go. There was an undefined darkness lurking
behind Minc's words.

Minc's black eyes were locked onto his as the boy demanded, "What's the matter with you? It's crazy, but I think
you're actually afraid of *me,* now. Afraid of what we are!
Well, I can show you—"

"Not another word, boy," Minor cut him off. "You've gone
too far with this. Way out of focus. The outside world isn't a
protected place like this installation, and children's games are
forbidden there. I admit, I experimented with those special
powers when I was growing up, too, but I was fortunate
enough to be forced to stop because using them would have
given me away. Besides, watching other people dance to my
orders sickened me. It went against my conscience. I made a

vow to myself, when I was younger than you are, never to touch those parts of my power again. Today, because of my position and the faith people put in me, the entire idea is repulsive. Those things are a child's toys, not a man's. You're a man now, so you'll have to relinquish them." He spat it out, letting it come harshly.

"When they're mine to use? Never! You're weak, Minor!" Minc condemned him. "And since you willingly gave up your chance, you have no claim to any part of mine when you see what I make of it. I'll stand alone! I always knew I did, anyway."

"Explain!" Minor ordered.

"Not one word's worth. This is where we're different—parent-cell—and I'm holding onto that difference. I *am* an individual, after all! Total-PSI or not, you're a zero like the rest of them."

Minor pushed himself up and strode across the room. He didn't want to hear this, or any more that might come. It shattered eighteen years—forty years—and it scared him. But it had to be faced.

He gave Minc one more chance. "Take some of those statements back, or explain your whole meaning. Otherwise, I won't be responsible for what I do."

Minc countered defiantly, "The meeting is over, Counselor. We'll see which one of us they clone the next time. The deciding factor will be weakness or strength, and I have the strength!"

Minor stopped still. This was too immense to let pass, and his silence flooded the room with a tension that reached out to push against the walls.

"All right, boy—*I'm coming*. Consent or not, trauma or not. Get ready to meet me, M-I-N-Clone! You're hiding things that are too big for hiding."

Minc whirled to run, but Minor was on him, crashing through his ego and down into his id, sucking up its essence, pulling at it brutally, repelled by it but forcing everything out. Never moving from his place, he attacked his Clone, and the boy fell against the door, receiving images in return—images *he* didn't want, either—images of Minor's past fear and insanity and loneliness.

After four minutes of absolute silence, Minor was through. He pulled his mind back, leaving Minc crumpled into himself. Minor turned away from the sight of him, sick to his stomach, and more than that—afraid.

So these were Minc's talked-of plans! No wonder he hadn't wanted to be probed. This boy was planning to destroy the world! And this boy could do it!

Minor gulped in air and crossed the room. He grasped Minc's shoulder and thrust him away from the door. "Get out of my way," he cursed at the boy. "I finally know you, and— I have nothing to say."

He left with Minc's telepathic shrieks in his mind. *"Don't leave me NOW, for God's sake! Don't! Help me! Please!"*

Minor didn't answer, but stamped on, letting the hard hit of his feet crush down the shock that was numbing his brain.

As he turned for his living quarters, he felt Minc's emotion change, going from horror to hatred, and Minc screamed, *"If this is how you want it, then all right! You'll never get out of my reach, you traitorous— You forced the lock-on between us, so you can suffer the results of it. I'll never let you rest again. I promise! Your wonderful dream begins NOW!"*

Refusing Ellis's company, Minor left the building and walked outside under the trees that surrounded it, hoping to bury himself in nature's peace, since he owned none of his own. Ellis trailed quietly behind, steady in his duty as body-guard but keeping out of the way.

No matter how Minor tried, there was no use attempting to think the experience through. Merging with his Clone had been shock enough, but what he had seen in that Clone was over-whelming, even if it finally proved to be only the revenge delusions of a misguided boy. His thoughts were an idiotic jumble; numbness and worry, disgust and pity. His brain seemed stuffed with cotton, refusing to let anything surface but Minc's dreadful cries of *"Help!"*

The boy was warped out of all sense, and floundering. He needed Minor's help, but Minor hadn't offered so much as a word. Because of the vileness he had seen in Minc, and the way it had distorted his anticipated dream, he had retreated al-together, leaving the boy to face his merging-shock alone. There was no excuse for such self-indulgence. He had to con-sider Minc. Nothing was coming from the boy now, and he wondered why. Had the visions of the merging been too much for him? Was he all right?

After two hours of walking aimlessly and finding none of the peace he'd come to gather, he stalled at one inescapable conclusion: Minc was right; he was traitorous. He had hit the boy with as much shock as he had experienced himself—slashed him into pieces—and then abandoned him. For all of his preconceived plans of guiding Minc through the trial of merging, he hadn't done it. Instead, he had betrayed him, and Minc's silence grew more ominous by the minute.

He yelled to Ellis, "I have to get back to my Clone!" and took off at a run.

A staff member gave him directions to Minc's bedroom, where she said the boy had holed up in his own turn. Before Minor could disappear into the maze of corridors, a hand touched his arm, and he swung around to find Ellis staring hard at him, his face red from running.

"What's happened?" Ellis panted, out of breath. "You've looked beleaguered for the last two hours, but you didn't give me a chance to ask why."

"I'm all right," Minor evaded. "It's just not every day that a man meets his own Clone."

"You two managed it, then? Good."

"No. It was as much of a shock to me as it was to him."

"Oh?" Ellis frowned. "Is it anything I can help you with?"

"Thanks, Ellis, but I have to do this for myself. No one can possibly help me." At Ellis's still unsatisfied expression, he tried to explain without revealing the truth. "Putting it simply, there still wasn't any joy in it. I feel as though I had drowned. So just be here, friend, and give me the chance to work it out. Right now, I have to find that boy!"

He clapped the younger man on the arm and turned away, heading straight for Minc. He located the designated room. Minc called, "Come in," when he knocked. He found the boy sitting cross-legged in the middle of a giant-sized bed, surrounded by a brightly decorated room that gave the impression of comfort and hominess. The only thing out of place was Minc's face. It was all one dark glare. He was disheveled, and the bed was a copy of him. He had obviously struggled on it in some violent burst of emotion.

"Why did you come back?" Minc asked aloud, staying clear of PSI.

Minor hunted for words. "To set things straight between us. To apologize for leaving you like that. I hurt you, and I had no right."

"Still crawling, Minor?"

"Don't do that, Minc. Don't turn me off before you hear what I'm saying. An apology isn't subservience."

"I know. You're 'thinking' it's decency."

Minor halted. Minc might be speaking aloud, but he was actually operating more deeply. Minor sighed. "Go ahead and probe me, Minc. Sponge up my emotions and motives. I don't care. I have no intention of going into you again until we've settled some things."

"What is there to settle?"

"One mountainous question. Why do you want to destroy the world?"

Minc smiled slyly, tilting his head so his dark hair fell across his forehead. "Because it's there?"

"I see. You won't answer. At least you aren't denying it."

"That would be a waste of time, and from now on I'm wasting no time, Minor. Since there's no place for you in my plans, I won't even discuss them with you."

Swallowing the retort that wanted out of him, Minor sat down in a blue-and-white-print chair. "That's just as well, because they're too big a subject, anyway. I'd rather start at the beginning—at the core of it. I want you to tell me something, Minc. Do you have any conscience at all? Any sense of morality?"

"You know everything I have, parent-cell. You gobbled it all up for yourself."

"Unfortunately, that's true. Then would you like to learn what morality is? To gain some basis for a judgment of whether or not it's a lack in you? You can't even decide against it until you know what it is."

"I don't need lessons. You've already taught me. Ethics and decency mean spouting off about never entering another person's mind without his consent, and then turning around and pouncing on him when the mood strikes you. I learn fast, Minor, and you're a good teacher. I'll grant you that much."

Minor stared at him blankly. "I can't seem to do anything right with you, can I? Nothing goes the way I plan it, and—"

"There you go, baring your soul again. I already know that, too. It's made up of crawling and fear and emptiness. A sickening picture. I want no part of it."

Old and remembered shame was the first thing that leaped into Minor, but he beat it down. His own devils weren't the reason for his being here. He blasted at the real ones. "Damn it, boy, I came back to help you! I walked out when you were in shreds and didn't offer to lead you through your shock. Is there anything you need of me now? Anything I can set straight in your mind? Anything I can ease?"

Minc's glare relented for a moment of hesitation, then returned full force. "You can relieve the clutter in my room by getting out, parent-cell. You've got these nauseating thoughts about showing me how to grow into a man, and offering me your strength. Get this straight, Minor—I don't need any of it. All I ever needed from you was instruction on how to do your work so I can leave this place. I got all of that in our 'loving' merging."

He switched jarringly to PSI that stabbed through Minor's brain. *"Get out, parent-cell, and don't bother to come back. I don't want you!"*

Minor forcibly kept himself from recoiling physically, and left the room on shaking legs. But he couldn't escape the rejection, because Minc's derision trailed him in telepathic stabs.

"Poor Minor—he wanted to be loved. The decent, stupid freak! Decent freak. Misfit weakling. Minor is a mis-fit; Minor is a mis-fit. Nobod-y loves Mi-nor."

It singsonged after him all the way to his quarters.

It was time to stop thinking about himself, or Minc, and begin tracking down possibilities. Giving way to self-pity wasn't going to help. Minor waited for the "empty-mind" feeling to signal that Minc wasn't tuned in to him and eavesdropping, and when it came after three torturous hours, he went to his bedroom and began to shoot questions at himself.

First, what exactly did Minc intend to do? The answer was too well remembered from the minutes of merging. Minc planned to leave this installation to work in the world as Minor was working, but not for the world's benefit. He wanted to gain complete domination over the Earth, make himself rich and honored and obeyed, and play out a few years wallowing in the proof that he *was* somebody, after all. Then, with all of Earth's weapons in his hands, he intended to destroy the planet and the people who populated it, taking his vengeance on the "zeros" who had been cruel enough to inflict the existence of a Clone on him. Before the actual destruction, he saw himself standing as a giant, with weapons tight in his hands, while the people begged him to let them survive.

It was an unhappy-boy's delusion, Minor was certain, and he had to accept the greater part of the guilt for that boy's unhappiness. He had wanted a Clone. True, he hadn't raised him to be lonely and unprincipled, but he had caused him to *be*. Now he had to "uncause" what Minc had become.

He pulled himself away from that line of thinking and back to the next real question. Could Minc carry out the first part of his plan? Could he maneuver himself into the position of control over the world's governments and set himself up as the prime authority? Even without Minor cooperating by doing part of it for him?

The answer required no effort, since all Minor really needed to consider was, "Could *I* do it?" His response was an obvious and frightening "Yes."

No one else was really aware of this capability in him.

Maybe it had crossed Stams's mind, but if so, Stams had buried it by holding short reins on him, as Ellis said, and Stams felt secure in his sense of control. But those reins would be worth no more than spider webs if Minor ever wanted to break free.

Minor paced to the window, staring out at the sunlit grass blindly. "Next question," he asked himself, *"how?"*

That answer was so simple it was laughable. Through thought control and hypnosis, Minc could come away from mediating sessions with every Ambassador his admiring pawn. By placing thoughts in their minds, he could convince them that he was wise, brilliant, and noble, even their world savior. He could manipulate them into clamoring for his election as their overriding ruler, a dictator with no opposition. Anywhere he traveled, every crowd of people could be nailed to his side just as easily. Then he'd have a planet-sized toy. Holding all the weapons, he would fondle the power of life and death over the people and the Earth itself. And, finally, decreeing death, he'd go down with them under his own fire.

Yes, the boy could do it. His own Clone—himself, in reality —could and would reap the world, and because of his bitterness, he'd use it meanly. A man who called everyone else a zero would treat them that way, and that's what they would ultimately become. Abused and—in the great hour of vengeance —killed.

The doing of it would mean Minc's death, too, and at this special moment, that was the threat that unnerved Minor. Everything else hinged on Minc anyway.

Minor shuddered and looked away from nature's light, then went further and closed it out entirely by drawing the drapes. The next question had to be posed in darkness, because it was the towering one.

He posed it directly, in the active mode, to bring it harshly home. "How can I stop him? In the short time I have, how can I teach him enough to save him from himself, and preserve him?"

His mind flicked in spasms across reflex ideas and was quickly entangled in them. When he couldn't surface a sensible approach, he gave up, aware that he was too shaken and depressed to think logically. He knew only that he had to awaken Minc to a sense of reality, penetrate his distrust, and divert him from his terrible fantasies before they gained so much momentum that they carried the floundering boy along with them. Somehow he must make Minc see that vengeance wasn't worth dying for, that it wasn't even appropriate, or necessary.

He rubbed his burning eyes and gave it up for the present. This kind of indecision would only tear him to pieces, and he had to hang onto his equilibrium. Ellis flashed to mind. The young man would be waiting in the living room, ready to offer companionship that would turn his mind to other things until it had rested enough to grapple with the problem. Ellis became a beacon that drew him toward the door.

Before he managed to open it and gain the light, Minc's PSI voice jarred inside his head. *"Minor is a mis-fit; what is Minor do-ing?"*

Minor slapped his hands flat on the closed door and dropped his forehead onto the cool wood. When had the boy tuned back in? How much of this soul-searching had he heard? He let his breath out in a great huff of futility, since it didn't matter anyway. Once thought, the ideas were forever in his brain, waiting for Minc to pluck at any time. If he had overheard enough of the last ones, perhaps they'd do him some good.

"Some good, some good," Minc echoed.

"Go on and play your singsong games," Minor responded. *"They don't bother me. From now on, you go into a cubby-hole of my brain labeled 'Pest.'"*

He straightened up and opened the door, the light flooding his face. He'd have to learn to live with Minc's taunts, because he knew the boy wouldn't stop them. Settling his fear for the Clone would be harder.

"Fear-fear-fear-fear," echoed from the inner part of the building. *"When are you going to sound the warning about me, Minor? Is Stams going to be the Chosen One? Bates is on my side, you know."*

"I'm not warning anyone, boy. This is solely between the two of us. A warning would give it credence and honor which it doesn't deserve. Keep on with your word games. I enjoy the company."

"Company-company-company-company—"

To hide his underlying thought of "You've jumped too fast, Minor; this is only a misguided boy's delusion," he joined in the game with Minc, saying in unison, *"Company-company-company—"* Minc was right again. Bates wouldn't listen to anything that spoke of imperfection in his prized Clone. And Stams? Stams might flare up in fear and go too far, even order Minc's destruction.

The last idea shook Minor harder than any of the others. No. The secret had to remain between the boy and himself. If Minc was to be saved, he had to handle it alone.

As his eyes lit on Ellis, he was suddenly confident. He could do it. Minc was just a boy, after all, and he'd never been shown strength on his own PSI level. No matter how he protested, there were conscience and sense in him, and Minor only had to find them. He would save Minc for himself, and the Earth for both of them. He was the only one who could. *"Only one, only one. Mis-fit Minor, Mis-fit Minor."*

A week passed with twice-a-day meetings between Minor and his Clone as Stams pressed Minor to speed up Minc's course of instruction. Minor accepted Stams's harrying but did no instructing. Instead, he used the meetings for his own purposes, persistently trying to break down the boy's stubbornness and touch his intelligence and emotion. Following any tack that occurred to him, he fought to drive home the truth of the danger, immorality, and ultimate suicide that lurked in Minc's plans. But he made no progress. Not even an inroad. Minc claimed he didn't care if he died. The way of his dying would make up for it.

With no flicker of success to encourage him, it was hell to be with the boy. He had prayed for another Total-PSI to share his existence, but he couldn't share anything with Minc, because Minc wasn't a separate person. Minc *was* Minor. Since they kept to the non-PSI level, they couldn't even converse satisfactorily, because their thoughts came at exactly the same instant, and they were forever beginning the same sentence with identical words in maddening synchronization. The only way to avoid it was to carefully slow and sort their ideas, or to deliberately keep to subjects that drew on the differences in their backgrounds, and Minc refused to cooperate with either of these methods very often.

So for Minor it was like conversing with his mirror image and watching his own mouth move as the man and the image spoke in unison. Sometimes Minc even spat out the words first, leaving Minor as a second-rate echo of his own ideas. Minc enjoyed watching him stammer and stop, reminding him of his complete rejection.

At least Minc had put aside his threats for the moment, secure in what he condemned as Minor's weakness and sure that Minor was no danger to him, but only a sensitive mind to torment. Minor took comfort from that. No word must ever leak out about Minc's deadly plans. Any such leak would jeopardize the boy's life. Stams and the government would assuredly order the Clone's death, and Minor couldn't endure the picture of a world without Minc in it. Not again. A tormentor or not, Minc belonged to him, and he desperately needed to protect him. Minc might not want him, but Minor had to have Minc.

As the days of failure dragged by, Minor's worry fattened into near panic. It happened because the boy was wearing him down. He had no chance to sleep or rest; no time to sustain even his physical strength, since Minc was constantly inside his brain, taunting and jeering, finally parroting Minor's every private thought. Even his dreams were duplicated, each picture reproduced one second after it appeared, making sleep impossible unless the boy was sleeping, too.

Now he wanted respite from his Clone as much as he'd fretted to be with him before. But he was cut off from gaining it by the awful premonition that if he admitted his reasons to anyone, he could be jeopardizing Minc's safety—or worse yet, endangering *their* sanity and even their lives. If he turned Minc "on" again without having found the way to turn him "off," Minc might retaliate against anyone he considered a threat.

His main emotion grew to be a sense of standing completely alone while he watched the approach of futility. He was too often eighteen again, hiding in a swarm of people, terrified of being torn apart.

At the end of the week, Stams sent an order to meet him in Bates's office. When he walked the corridors, the parroting

Minc was with him, as he had been for a steady thirty-six hours.

"Where are you going, Minor?"

"You know as well as I do."

"You know as well as I do," Minc echoed. *"Where?"*

"All right." Minor sighed mentally. *"Dr. Stams wants to see me."*

"Dr. Stams wants to see me."

"And I don't really need you along."

"And I don't really need you along."

"Cut it—!" Minor chopped the thought in two. *"Would it do me any good to say please?"*

". . . any good to say please?"

"Forget I said it," Minor told him, reaching out to knock on Bates's door.

"Forget I said it."

A woman's voice called, "Come right on in! There's no need to knock," and when Minor entered, he realized he'd made the ridiculous mistake of knocking at Bates's *outer* office, so he was facing the doctor's receptionist. Embarrassed, he mumbled, "I must have my head on backwards, or something."

". . . my head on backwards, or something."

The young woman laughed. "Your mind is just somewhere else, Counselor Minor. It happens to all of us eventually."

"Somewhere else, indeed!" Minor grunted to himself.

"Somewhere else, indeed!" Minc repeated.

The receptionist was saying, ". . . so you can go right in. They're waiting for you."

"They?"

"They?"

"Dr. Bates and Dr. Stams. Weren't you expecting both of them?"

"*. . . expecting both of them?*"

"Don't start in on what *other* people say, too!" Minor answered Minc aloud.

The receptionist's head cocked, startled.

"I'm sorry," he told her. Minc was unbalancing him. "I don't know . . ."

"Are you all right, Counselor?" she asked with concern.

"Yes, thank you, really. I'll go in. . . . I'll go on in now."

He hurried to the inner door, Minc still parroting. "*I'll go on in now.*"

Stams stood up at Minor's entrance, and his brows immediately drew down. "What in the devil's name has happened to you?" he demanded. "It's been only two days since I've seen you, but you look as though you'd been on a six-day binge!"

"And feel like it," Minor admitted. "What do you want? I don't have the patience for any browbeating, so . . ."

"*. . . any browbeating, so . . .*"

"We're after a report, naturally," Bates said. "You haven't given us anything significant since you've been here. From the look of you, something significant has been happening."

"If you call being pestered to death significant, then yes, it has!" Minor snapped. "If I have the chance to push any words over the top of your expensive little parrot, maybe I can explain."

"*. . . maybe I can explain.*"

"*Will you shut up?*" Minor exploded at his Clone. "*This whole conversation will be about you, so you'll enjoy it. Let it be, boy!*"

"*Make it good and I'll give you King's X,*" Minc answered, at last in his own words.

To the doctors, Minor said. "I have a complaint, and I want it noted down loud and clear! If you have any control over the Clone, Bates, use it! The boy is after me day and night. He mimics every word I say or think, and I'm about ready to strangle him to keep him quiet!"

He waited for Minc to echo, but the King's X remained blessedly in effect.

"By 'all night,' I assume you mean you've had no sleep," Stams said. "That accounts for the deterioration of your face?"

"Black circles, exhausted wrinkles, and all." Stams had taken the direction Minor wanted. He'd focused on the small evil so Minor could conceal the big one.

"Mimicry, is it?" Bates smiled, trying to picture it as a PSI process.

"Exactly," Minor said.

Stams nodded wisely. "All children go through it at one time or another. If you ask, 'Would you like some candy?' they say, 'Would you like some candy?' I've had it done to me. It's exasperating, but harmless. A child's game. Of course, the children are usually younger than eighteen."

"So?" Bates bridled. "Minc isn't emotionally mature. I've told you that before." He turned to Minor. "When children get into this game it's distracting, certainly, but not intolerable."

Out of his frustration at ever making Normals understand anything to do with PSI, Minor challenged, "If they say the words before you do? If they think them as you do and say them a millisecond later? You can't know what it's like, and I can't stand it!"

"Then ask the boy to stop," Bates soothed.

"I have, and he won't! He's enjoying himself. Worse, right now, while I'm admitting how he bothers me, he's hearing every word I say, plus the ones I'm not saying. I had managed to keep my dignity until now, but this confession will give him all the satisfaction he needs to keep harping at me."

Stams was at an obvious loss. "He'll tire of it. Outgrow it. He's too intelligent to stick to foolishness of this kind."

"In other words, 'Go handle it yourself, Minor, because it's in your own weird milieu.' That's what I expected to be told."

"Why must I constantly ask you to calm yourself, Counselor?" Stams demanded. "In all of our years together, we've never had arguments, but since you arrived here, you've been nothing but belligerent."

"I've kept my mouth shut all these years, Stams, and that's the truth of it. Just put today's poor behavior down to exhaustion, and let me go back to my rooms. I've given all the report I have to give, and I'm too tired to be badgered."

Stams eyed him closely. "Whatever you say—for the moment. Except that I want you to check with the medical doctor, Ramison, for an examination. Your physical condition and agitation worry me. It's disquieting to see a strong man collapsing."

"I'll do it, if only to get some knock-out drops. A few hours of peace are all I need. And don't worry about your Clone, Bates. Whatever has to be done, Minc and I will work it out between us."

"Right, Minor," Stams said. "Have patience and handle him."

"Of course. He's my own weird milieu, too. Report finished."

As Minor fled for the door, Minc asked, *"You're not going any further? You're not going to tell them how dangerous I am?"*

"I told you I wasn't. What could they do about you, anyway?"

"True. Good Minor. Sensible Minor."

"Go to sleep, Minc. You have to be tired."

"Go to sleep, Minc. You have to be tired."

Minor let Minc play, rage, and torment, mustering determination to keep himself from breaking down, exhausted or not.

The sleeping pills only chained him to the boy's dream-parroting, so he gave them up as useless. But Minc wasn't going to defeat him. Not this easily. Not when both of their futures were hanging on Minor's actions.

Making a point of sleeping when Minc slept, or at any time the boy tuned away from him, he returned his physical appearance to a passable condition. He even withstood Stams's proddings to hurry with the teaching and get the boy ready so that Stams could reap the glory of announcing the Clone to the world as a second Minor, a second buffer against disaster. The cloning itself, plus the eighteen years of protected living, had been expensive, and an accounting was due. Minor let Stams batter at him, unheeded, as he frantically searched for a way to stop Minc, stealing a half hour here and there when Minc was tuned out to run down his own ideas.

It was all closing in, in spite of everything he tried. Minc was impatient. He insisted that he had learned everything he needed about mediation-monitoring and disaster-forecasting and was ready to leave his confinement. Minor's time for action was short, and shrinking. The more eager the two-faced Clone became, the more irrational Minor's pleas for time appeared to be.

The day Stams sent directly for Ellis was a shock.

After Ellis left their shared quarters, Minor fought with his conscience and lost. Ellis belonged with him; Ellis was his last hope for aid, and now Stams had called him away. Needing to know "why" for his own protection, Minor opened his mind and jumped it into their conversation, barrelling from Ellis's brain to Stams's, garnering each word spoken and every reacting emotion.

The gleanings upset him. Stams ordered Ellis to play a new role—watchdog for a supposedly cracking Minor. Ellis's reaction was the worst of it. The young man recoiled. Minor didn't wait to see whether it was against the idea of being a spy or from the possibility that Minor was losing his grip on reality. He withdrew his mind from the office and left them to their conspiracies, feeling unreasonably dirty for eavesdropping.

"Ethics, Minor, are all-important," Minc put in his voice. *"But you jump back and forth across them without ever touching the middle you insist is so honorable. The lesson for today is Pretense."*

"Go away," Minor told him. *"You claim to have no conscience, so you can't judge."*

"Don't be nasty to your little Clone. I'm going. I don't need to stay now, because you have Ellis to watch you. Everybody thinks you're going crazy. Fun? I'll tune out and let you be lonely. Miss me, Minor. I'm the other half of your populated world, and I'm leaving it."

Minor checked an impulse to cry, "No! Stay!"

Minor's reprieve lasted exactly twelve hours. Then Minc was back, shouting inside Minor's brain. Minor read his new motive empathically, and it was evil. To Minc, the logic was simple; if Minor was the only block to his escape from these walls, and if Minor was on the verge of collapse, then shove Minor over the edge by pushing him into exhaustion.

There was no sleep that night, and Minor had counted on it, stealing no rest during the day. He spent the next physical meeting with the boy just sitting and staring at him, constantly jolted by Minc's threats that he'd soon be free to begin his great plan. There seemed to be no way to save him from himself.

After two more of those meetings, Minor gave up. He couldn't handle Minc. Why had he ever thought he could? No man could completely control himself. He was going to lose Minc, one way or another. The only fact he knew for certain was that he wouldn't betray the boy. He had done that already —at the moment of his cloning.

Once he let the problem go as too enormous to hammer down, he fell into a state of preoccupation, grieving silently as he listened to Minc's taunts. He mumbled weak excuses for his depression whenever Ellis cornered him out of concern for his haggardness, because he wasn't sure he could trust even Ellis anymore. After all, Ellis was Stams's man, and Stams was more and more certain that Minor was losing his sanity.

On a dismal, sunless Wednesday, Stams broke in on the session between Minor and his Clone. He smiled at Minc, then immediately confronted Minor with, "Don't give me a word of protest, Counselor. I came to see for myself what goes on in here. And what do I find? Silence."

"What else did you expect when two PSIs are together?" Minor was irritated by the intrusion.

"All right, I'll grant you that. But I have a direct question, and this time I'm demanding a direct answer. Are you finished with the boy's instruction, or aren't you? You've had more than enough time, according to your own promises, and he says you are."

Minor was empty of arguments. Minc had obviously been reporting to Stams behind his back, and it was the truth, anyway. Minc did have all the knowledge he needed.

Stams caught Minc's smirk at the exact moment Minor "felt" triumph radiating from the boy. Surprisingly, Stams deferred to Minor—whether out of habit or out of uneasiness with the boy's smile, Minor didn't know. "What's he looking so smug about, Counselor?"

"He knows he's won," Minor answered. "He picked it out of my brain that I was ready to admit he's fully tutored, and that . . ."

". . . you have what you need in him, so you don't need me

anymore." The last half of Minor's sentence came out of Minc's mouth, but not exactly as Minor had intended to finish it. The Clone even added Minor's unspoken thoughts of, "Take the boy and be damned. I only want some peace. I can't live like this."

Stams swiveled from one to the other of them, his jaw slack. "What's going on? Minc speaks for you, now?"

"Why not?" Minor shrugged. "He *is* me! You created a man with a three-dimensional shadow. Except that the shadow is malevolent." It was a relief to say it.

Stams was immediately deaf. "Now come on, Minor, that's illogical. If he *is* you, then he's just like you, and you've never been—"

"He's me, all right, but he's not like me. He didn't have to . . ."

". . . control himself, or take the hard blows that would have knocked the power hunger out of him," Minc finished for Minor again. Then he laughed and spoke for himself, following along with Stams's approach. "You're ridiculous, Minor. I'm not the one who's out of step. It's you! You've never had the good sense to accept what we are."

"Don't say 'we'!" Minor said. "Don't ever say it again!"

They faced each other, eyes dark, and Stams hurried nervously out of their way. "I don't understand any of this. Someone has turned this place into a madhouse! But I'm returning to my original question, Counselor. Is the boy ready, or isn't he? After this demonstration of his powers, I'd say he is, and that's the only matter of importance."

Minor stared at Stams and smiled slyly. "Give him a Mediating Session to monitor, some Ambassadors to probe, and see what he does."

Stams backed up, uncomfortable with Minor's inflection. "I think that's the most sensible thing you've said. You two get back to whatever it was you were doing." He swung around and left, visibly shaken.

"Thank you, Counselor," Minc said.

"I had nothing to do with it. You *are* ready, and . . ."

". . . there's no denying me. That's not what I was thanking you for. I was glad to see you turn on your backriding Dr. Stams. But you're too late. This is where we part company. I go up, and you go down."

"The parting is all that interests me," Minor said. "I don't want to watch you kill yourself. You're so young, Minc."

"You say that, but you're thinking, 'Have I betrayed the world?' I'll give you the answer. Yes, you have. Out of your own stupidity and weakness. Look at yourself. Where is all that strength you offered me to lean on?"

Minor didn't answer. Even his mind was a blank.

"I shouldn't be so cruel, should I?" Minc pretended to relent. "So then, here I stand for you to lean on, Minor. My strength is greater than it ever was. You'll see it's true when I show the rest of the zeros in the world. You'll beg right along with them, Minor. On your knees."

Minor stared at the boy, and hatred started grinding in his soul. Where it came from, he didn't know, but it was there. "You're not out of here yet, Clone."

Minc laughed. "You're right. And that brings up my final point. You tried to turn a corner with Stams. You stopped protecting me and tried to edge in a warning. I covered it by befuddling him enough so it didn't register, but you have to be silenced, Minor. The play is all mine now, and you can't raise any blocks against me. Not even any delays."

"Forget your threats, Minc. You're harmless when it comes to me. It amounts to trying to silence yourself. Remember that."

Minc still laughed. Then his black eyes darted sideways to the bookcase, and a heavy volume vibrated on the shelf. It jumped free, and before Minor realized what was happening, the eight pounds of dead weight hurtled for his head.

He ducked, and it crashed into the wall, cracking and dropping plaster. He clenched his fists in reflex, visualizing the broken plaster as his head. The Clone had tried to kill him! Using PSI power only, he had transformed an everyday object into a weapon and hurled it to split Minor's skull!

"Yes!" Minc spat the word telepathically. *"And I won't miss again!"*

A bronze statue leaped off a side table and zoomed at Minor. Formed like a Roman soldier, it brandished a jutting six-inch spear that came arrowing for Minor's right eye.

In the breathless moment of its onrush, Minor fixed it with his mind, feeling his invisible PSI hands encircle it in midair and jerk it to a halt.

But it didn't fall. It hung there, threatening to come on again as Minor's PSI hands were grabbed by Minc's, and they grappled mentally with the weapon. It hovered between them, swaying forward and back, forward and back, testing their strength to decide its path.

Minc's PSI was incredibly strong, and Minor had to hunch his shoulders to gather force against it. The spear still pointed at his eye as he inhaled a grating breath—and twisted the statue in his mind.

It turned.

Now the spear was a danger to Minc, and the boy leaned toward it, his mind pushing to fling it away. But it didn't move, and Minor's second hoarse breath started it inching back the way it had come, closer and closer to the Clone.

Minc watched it gain speed, straining to stop it. As Minor sensed the boy's struggle, he coiled his PSI energy into a fist and hit the statue with a shove that freed it from the battle and sent it flying at its target.

Minc's eyes flared and a cry of "No!" rasped out of him. His fear changed to panic, and he released his "holding" grasp to deal a crushing, downward PSI blow. The statue thumped to the floor with a bang that jarred the room.

Minor stumbled three steps forward as his body reacted as though it had been pushing at the fallen object physically. He and Minc stood staring at the statue, then Minor walked over and picked it up. Minc's emotions were open to him and came in a terrible jam of fright and heightened resentment. The boy had tested himself against his "parent" and proved to be lacking.

Minor held his head higher because of it. He wasn't merely an object for this boy's ridicule and manipulation, and finally Minc had to accept that fact.

"Do you really believe you proved all that much?" Minc demanded, regaining his poise. Now his emotion was shot through with hatred. "Don't be a fool and think you're safe, parent-cell. You're feeling a little pride, but just find a mirror and you'll see the truth. You're pitiable! A dilapidation of a man."

Minor caught himself self-consciously trying to straighten his clothing and stopped short. Hatred beat in his own heart, and he let it grow because it was hot and true.

"You tried to kill me, Clone!"

"Why not?" Minc answered. "You're through, parent-cell. Lie down and admit it. You can't save me from myself any more than you've ever been able to save yourself from yourself. Everything is just as it was, and it's mine for the taking. Stams still thinks you're crazy, and I'm still ready to become the world's new defender." He laughed again, a laugh that was, if possible, more evil as a PSI sound than it had ever been aloud.

Minor walked out on it. Let Minc eavesdrop on his—let Minc do whatever he wanted to do. Minor had his own duty now. He'd failed to change the Clone's mind for one reason only: the Clone was insane! Paranoidal! He couldn't let his hand be stayed by pity or guilt any longer, because the world was hanging around his neck, and the world had to be protected.

If there was even one shot left in the battle, he'd take it. He was ready to admit it all to Stams and beg for help before it was too late.

Minor slammed into Bates's office without knocking, and both doctors jerked upright, startled. He didn't give them time to utter a question.

"I've come to make my report," he said flatly. "And to hand you a giant crisis. You won't like what I'm going to say, but you have to hear it, so get ready. If you have any idea of turning that Clone loose on the world, forget it right now, because he plans to make the Earth his private ground and let the devil take anyone who stands in his way. He's going to dominate it, rape it, and then destroy it!"

"Wha—?" Bates was halfway out of his chair.

"No questions. Just listen," Minor ordered. "I don't have any solutions. I don't know what you can do with him or how you can stop him, but you have to try. Your pampered, experimental baby is going to eat up the world!"

The sudden denouncement was too much for Bates to cope with, but Stams remained cool. He assumed an overly calm tone and moved to take control. "Counselor Minor, I think the best course is for you to sit down and take hold of yourself.

After what I saw between you and the boy a while ago—well, you're obviously overwrought. You're not making sense."

"I'm warning—"

"No more, no more," Stams cut him off. "Cool down, and we'll hear you out and discuss this rationally. What's disturbing you this time? Is it the new tack Minc has taken? This business of finishing your sentences for you?"

"No! That amounts to nothing! I could do it when I was ten! The point is, I *didn't*. I'm not here to complain. I'm begging for help with—"

"He's driving you wild with this new game, is that it?" Bates followed along with Stams.

They were humoring him! Minor couldn't let it continue, but how was he to get around it? He tried with, "If you insist on sticking to that subject, all right. I'll explain what I have to say from *that* starting point. I could do all of the same pestering things that Minc can do—all of them—but I didn't, because I couldn't risk it. I would have given myself away immediately.

"Minc has been raised like a young emperor, so he doesn't to this day understand anything about morality or decency. You didn't bother to teach him, and I wasn't allowed access to him. Consequently, you raised an egomaniac who thinks he deserves to own the world. He even wants me out of the way so he can stand above everyone as the giant he thinks he is. He's doing his best to kill me out of jealousy, hatred, and an insatiable greed to have it all for himself. To be the only one of 'us' alive." He realized at once that he'd gone too far, letting the dammed-up emotions overflow. But they couldn't be taken back.

Bates's response proved he was right. "The insanity of your accusations shows so clearly that even you should be able to see it, Counselor. Minc couldn't possibly kill you by using PSI."

"Then how about a heavy, pointed statue? Hurled at my face?"

"He did that?" Stams was finally listening.

But Bates gave Minor no chance to press the small turn toward his side. "I won't believe such a thing if you shout it at me all day, Minor. Minc can't want to kill you. He *is* you."

"He is not me! He has my face and body and PSI powers, but that's as far as the likeness goes. His environment made the difference. Whether you like hearing it or not, Bates, you've raised a monster!" Speaking the word aloud to another human being rocketed his first fear through him again.

"He's only a boy," Bates defended his own.

"A monster! A paranoidal monster, monster, *monster!* And you have to find the way to control him!"

Stams motioned Bates down. He seemed willing to listen, but Minor knew most of it was pretense to ease his anxiety at seeing his supposedly "leashed" PSI man so violent. "Tell us all of it, Counselor. And with the panic erased from your face, please."

"My face!" Minor shot back. "It's in my guts, man!" He had to make them understand, but for some reason he was gaining no headway. He controlled his voice and said, "That Clone and I merged minds at our second meeting—because I forced it. He didn't accept me willingly."

"You made him do it?" Bates didn't like the sound of it.

"That's how I found out what he is. What he wants to be!" He cast his eyes back to Stams. "Bates has let the Clone run wild with his powers, and he's enjoyed it. He still does. He believes he's all-powerful. Add to that his bitterness at being nothing more than a Clone, and you have an unbalanced mind with delusions of owning the world simply to prove that he *is* somebody—then making the world idolize him and give him its treasures until he tires of that kind of power and reaches for the ultimate one. Life and death. He envisions himself standing alone with all the people of the Earth on their knees, begging him not to destroy them—right up to the glorious moment when he fires off the weapons, letting the screams for mercy literally die in his ears. They're delusions, yes, but it's not that simple. He can make them come true!"

"Really, now—" Bates began a denial.

"Take your 'really nows' and go back into your laboratory hole, Bates. Or better yet, ask me what I could do with the world if I wanted to. How I could make you think what I wanted you to think, how I could force people to act the way I wanted them to act; how I could fashion myself into a total dictator! You've raised a boy with those exact goals in mind, and God help us, I don't see how we can stop him!"

Silence hung at the end of his speech, and in that silence he knew he had again gone too far. He had let all of his desperation of the past days spew out of him, leaving him shaking. Stams's severe stare underlined it.

"Do you need a tranquilizer?" Stams asked.

"What?" Minor stabbed his black eyes at the shorter man. "Don't you dare even suggest—"

"Then get yourself in hand so we can talk this out. You're raving! I know you, Counselor. I was the first government psychiatrist to examine you after you collapsed—insane—on the street. I never expected such a flare of ranting in you again, but you've clearly undergone great emotional shock. I insist that you subdue yourself before it gets out of hand."

"Before you lose control entirely," Bates said, fidgeting.

"Quit being afraid of me, Bates!" Minor lashed out at him. "I'm not on the verge of going berserk. There's not enough intelligence in this room worth the taking, anyway. That's undoubtedly the reason Minc has bided his time. And just because Stams finally came right out and labeled me 'insane' eighteen years ago doesn't mean I was."

"Sit down!" Stams ordered.

Minor stayed still for a long moment, then surrendered that much ground. If his being in a relaxed-looking posture would make them listen, he was ready to lie on the floor. None of this was going his way. He'd lost all dignity and respect in their eyes, and he had to get it back.

"Now," Stams began, his voice firm and carrying a clinical edge, "you say that you and the boy made the merging at your second meeting."

"Yes."

"Will you concede that it was a traumatic experience for you?"

"Traumatic! It scared the insides out of me! I wasn't prepared for what I found. He's—"

"So we have an admitted case of emotional upheaval on your part," Stams overrode him. "The experience put you off balance. We made you wait eighteen years for it—building it up in your mind—and when it came, it overwhelmed you. You see, Counselor? When you view it objectively, it's very simple. Misinterpretation of what you experienced in that merging, plus the boy's subsequent harassing, have to be the reasons for these wild accusations. Because none of them is believable."

"Your mental blocks aren't believable, either," Minor said. "Have you spent too much money to admit you've produced a monster?"

"Minc is not a monster." Bates spoke freely for the first time, defending his prize. "When I hear you call him that, I think Dr. Stams should add one more factor to your trauma. Jealousy! You met your Clone, found him to be as capable as you are—perhaps more capable because of his careful upbringing—and you're unwilling to give him room. You're afraid to share your special place in the world."

Minor couldn't believe any of it. He had hurried in here to sound a terrible alarm and ask for help, but instead of listening, they were analyzing him. "That Clone wants everyone's place in the world. Can't you see that?"

Bates was adamant. "The idea is preposterous. I know the boy."

"Sure you do. One face. I know his soul."

Stams oddly moved away from him, placing Bates's desk between himself and Minor, before he said, "Even so, let's go on with this in Dr. Bates's way for a while, Counselor. If your statements aren't the result of trauma or jealousy, why didn't any of this come out of you before? Why did you wait until the boy was ready to leave and start his work?"

"Because I was covering for him," Minor said in a low voice. "I admit it. I was trying to work with him, to save him from himself and for myself. It turned out that he only wanted me as a tool to get him out of here and into the Mediating Sessions—as a teacher to help him direct his powers. I wanted him so much that I blinded myself to his insanity and endangered the world.

"That selfishness is the hardest part of this confession. But, believe me, I was sure I could change him—that he only needed one of his own kind to straighten him out. To help him. Because he didn't have to be this way." He looked at the floor because their uncaring faces were on the brink of wringing the next words out of him in sobs. "He can't be saved. I hate the fact as I say it, but he can't be saved."

Even Stams was affected by the emotion, but he quickly hid it by continuing in his clinical vein as though it hadn't been said. "The next thing I must know, Minor, is whether you can honestly claim that you're capable of controlling, and then destroying, the world."

"I am," Minor said simply. Then he calmly explained what he had thrashed out for himself about the use of thought control and hypnosis at the Mediating Sessions and about gaining control of Earth's men and weapons. "I could destroy the Earth, just as the Clone will."

"But don't you see how irrational that is, Minor? Minc would die, too. He'd never do that to himself."

"You're wrong, Dr. Stams. He doesn't care about his own death, and that's the proof of his insanity. Look at the cases of assassins. They're usually aware that their act will be their death, but they don't care. They only want the glory—the spotlight. He'll be the *world's* assassin!"

"But he has no reason for such terrible desires."

"He does, and I understand them, even if you don't. You isolated him, so he grew up alone, just as I did. But you also pampered him and never stopped to consider that he might resent being a Clone and being so alone. Instead of having to conform to the world, he focused his hatred on it, beginning with you, Bates. You offered him a focal point which I never had. I was alone in a vast population and never thought of blaming anyone for my condition. But Minc homed in on you and your staff—his little world—and got it into his head that you 'manufactured' him to be a nothing. From that twisted starting point, he generalized that all Normals are heartless and deserve to be destroyed—after they first see how truly outstanding he is. He's willing to die for that vengeance."

Minor felt he had put it well and calmly, but after some moments Stams said, "If he were willing to die that way, then he would be insane, as you say. But I can't go along with you, Minor. You're throwing your own distorted conception of yourself onto him. I'm not even convinced that you have the power to grasp control of the world. Nothing in your history has ever hinted at such power."

Frustration flared in Minor again. His careful self-control and logical presentation hadn't made a dent. He growled, "I possess powers you don't even know about, because your puny Telepaths can't get deep enough into my brain to find them."

"Since when?"

"No! Let all of that go!" Minor was suddenly waving them off, gesturing for silence to track down a facet of the plot he hadn't dredged up before. He spoke it aloud, as it came, excitedly throwing the words out with a premonition that these were going to turn into something to force them to listen.

"The ultimate fact that should be scaring the hell out of you is something *I* haven't even touched on before this minute. Think about this. If I did decide to use my PSI power for my own ends—the Clone's ends—how could I be stopped? By exposure, imprisonment, assassination? No! I'd automatically be aware of any plot against me, because the very existence of a plot means someone is carrying the idea in his head, and the human brain is a sieve to me. It drains out its thoughts with no prayer of closing its holes. I'd instantly be aware of any plot against me, and move to put it down. Who could imprison me when I have thought control to protect myself? Who could attack me?"

Minor stopped, his eyes wide but blank. He dropped his head into his hands with a groan, thinking, "Good God, so could Minc! What earthly use is any of this when no one can even scratch him?"

At that exact instant he heard a laugh, a mocking, arrogant laugh that was planted in the convolutions of his brain, but wasn't his. Minc was laughing at his helplessness.

"Get out of my head, you—" Minor screamed back at him, but he was cut off by a PSI threat of—

"I can't, parent-cell. You locked us together forever. Where you go, I go, and it's not going to be nice for you."

Stams's anxious voice erased the silent one. "Are you ill?"

"To death." Minor lifted his head and looked at them. They were honestly worried about him now, but it didn't matter anymore whether they believed what he'd said, since they were powerless to do anything about it.

"Get out of there, parent-cell, before you make a bigger fool of yourself," Minc said inside his head.

"Yes, I'd better," Minor heard his own voice speak hoarsely.

"What did you say?" Stams clutched the protection of the desk more closely.

"Uh, just— I'd better go." Minor lurched to his feet.

"Perhaps you should lie down." Bates was suddenly solicitous. "This entire experience has been too much for you, I'm afraid. With rest, you'll see how mistaken your conclusions are."

"Don't ever believe that, Doctor," Minor told him. He slumped into himself, his last shred of fight gone as he saw Bates's expression remain fixed. He sighed. "Am I right in judging the opinion in this room to be that I'm either jealous of Minc, or afraid of him, or on my way to another mental collapse? Are those my choices?"

"I don't see any others," Bates answered.

Minor swung his head wearily to Stams.

"If you'd take a close look at yourself, Counselor, you'd understand," Stams said. "You're a ghost of the man who came here."

"My physical appearance doesn't count for a damn. But neither of you comprehends that, so I won't argue anymore. There's nothing to argue about, anyway. You'll have to play this thing out until you prove for yourselves what I've said.

Only, by then, you probably won't even be aware of what's happened to you."

Minor moved for the door, his knees empty in their sockets making him lurch.

Stams grabbed for the office phone. "I'll send for Ellis to help you back to your rooms."

"Don't bother. I won't be walking alone. I never am, anymore."

He left them with that confusing statement, sure that Stams would alert Ellis anyway.

"You put on a big act, but they didn't believe it, did they?" echoed inside his brain. *"Now all that's left is for you to prove how right their diagnosis is. But you told them one piece of truth, parent-cell. Neither of us will ever be alone again."*

Ellis met him at the door and led him to his bed, but there was no rest to be found. He lay prone for four hours, but the darkness couldn't blot out the threatening PSI calls that poured out of Minc. He had no chance to think for himself and decided it was just as well, since all he had to think about was the deadly mistake he'd made in not telling Stams the truth immediately, while he was still a figure of strength and rationality. Perhaps he would have been believed then.

The result would have been the same, however. There was only one man on Earth who had a prayer of dealing with the Clone, and now that man was nearly incapable of dealing with anything. Oddly, he felt a sense of not caring anymore. He was empty. So he gave himself over to the Clone and let the boy think for him. Everyone insisted that Minc was him, so why not surrender to it?

At the end of the four hours of floating on Minc's mind, something new crept in. Emotion. Planted, manufactured, and false emotion that took seed in his own brain's memory and multiplied itself into a vibrating thing that shook his body.

Insecurity. Loneliness. Fear. He was eighteen again, with all that being eighteen meant to him. Wandering through crowds of people with a desperate need to hide, and finding no place to hide.

Shame. He was a freak; concealed for the moment, but bound to be discovered and shamed in front of the world, then destroyed for the danger he presented. He felt dirty, huge, and painfully visible, when all he wanted was to be tiny and safe in some dark corner. Whom was there to trust? Not a soul or spirit anywhere. Not even himself, because he might accidentally give himself away and become his own executioner as he was his own devil.

A vivid image clamped onto him of a street with a figure shambling along it, jostled by the crowd, the mouth moving as it mumbled nonsense phrases. Such strong pity rose in him for that figure that tears seeped out of his eyes. With their coming, and the vast, compassionate emotion, he was horribly inside the figure—he was the figure—himself—Minor—eighteen, and going mad!

He struggled to sit up, flailing the air in front of his eyes to bash down a mental picture that wouldn't even crack. He couldn't live that moment again! He couldn't bear to feel it again!

There was a loud sound within him, and somewhere in a sane recess of his mind he knew it was his own voice, screaming for help, screaming nothing-words—screaming!

The bedroom light flashed up, and Ellis was there, too, barely visible and standing immobile—Ellis and the street together, focusing and refocusing, back and forth, one into the other, both blurred. He thrust out his hands to Ellis, letting his mouth scream uncontrolled, unable to form a sensible word, but crying desperately inside, "Help me!"

Then Ellis had hold of his hands and was on the bed with him, his strong arms around Minor's quivering body, and Ellis was shouting, but it was all incomprehensible over the rantings of that figure he was "inside of" on the street, and the figure was falling—falling—the cement rising up to crash into it.

He waited for the impact eagerly, because on the other side of it lay blessed unconsciousness and peace. He held his breath expectantly as the cement came for his face.

It stopped an inch away.

Inside the figure of himself, he hung suspended nearly parallel to the sidewalk, with the violent emotions of the fall surging through him with no release.

"Breathe!" he heard Ellis calling faintly.

But he couldn't. He was capable only of emotion and was hanging in a giant mass of it; the insane, babbling emotion of a mind gone to shatters.

It blanked out.

As suddenly as it had come, the image of the eighteen-year-old disintegrated, and Minor was jerked back to the lighted room, the bed, and Ellis's strong arms. He was clutching Ellis with the strength of ten madmen. It was over. Over! He panted, his lungs tight from the lack of air.

"At last!" Ellis sighed. "Minor—what—?"

"It's all—all right." Minor let go of the young man. "A nightmare. A terrific bash of a nightmare."

Ellis's blue eyes scanned his face closely. "It must have been a horror of a one, because it even scared me. Do you need Dr. Stams?"

"No! No," Minor toned down the word. "I'm entitled to some erratic behavior without Stams's analyzing." He quieted his anger and confessed, "These last weeks haven't been easy, Ellis."

"I know. I've been worried for you. I still am, Counselor."

"Don't be. Just stay close and hang on, as I'm doing. We'll be leaving here soon."

"You've finished teaching your Clone?" Ellis was as relieved at the possibility of leaving as Minor was.

"He's ready to go it alone. And so am I, Ellis. So am I. So am I."

"You haven't talked to me about it—no one has—but things didn't turn out the way you dreamed, did they?"

Minor gazed at him silently, close to despair as he felt sympathy being offered for the first time in so very long. "Dreams are for Normals, Ellis. They die too fast when you're like me and can see the bottom of them. Dreams need mystery to stand on, and imagination to keep them in one piece. When you know the whole truth, there's no dream left."

Ellis didn't answer. He didn't like the statement or the isolation it implied, but he couldn't refute it. Not Normal Ellis. After a long moment he said, "I'll stay near, Counselor. I won't leave you alone again. I won't even leave the room while you sleep, if you think you may have another nightmare."

Ice pierced through Minor as he realized that the image of his eighteen-year-old self could come again. He knew full well what it had been. Minc had begun his attack. The Clone was going to drive him back into insanity. To destroy him.

"It's a lot to ask of you, Ellis, but I'm going to ask it." Ellis's presence had helped pull him back from that hallucination of collapse. By presenting a second image, it had prevented him from immersing himself so deeply that he couldn't climb back out.

"I'll sit up in the chair, then," Ellis told him. "If you need me, I'll be only four steps away."

Overriding Ellis's comforting words came a PSI shriek. *"Can it come again, parent-cell? Will it come again? The flexing of mental muscles with a statue is one thing; but a past with insanity in it is another. Go to sleep, Minor-parent-cell. I'll see you in your dreams."*

Minor lay back against the pillow, sickeningly aware of his final mistake. The statue. The incident should have ended in a stalemate, with the weapon dropping to the floor. He shouldn't have sent it back toward the Clone and proved himself stronger simply because of his maturity. By frightening Minc, he had triggered the boy's move into the awful pursuit of his plans.

But, at the time, Minor hadn't stopped to think. He had been occupied with trying to save his own life.

"You lost it anyway, parent-cell. Unless the existence of a maniac is what you'll call 'Life' when you wind up in it."

For the rest of the day and all thorough the night, Minc kept after him, but Minor didn't let himself relax enough to "float," so the boy's projected images were horrors, but they never caught him off guard again. He fought back, wearing himself thin, but refusing to surrender to Minc's onslaught.

At nine o'clock the next morning, Minc abruptly left Minor's mind, and his absence was almost tangible. In the relief he couldn't fully enjoy because of his exhaustion, Minor let Ellis order him a substantial breakfast and downed it automatically for its nourishment, not its flavor. He made no pretense of attending another meeting with the Clone, but remained adamantly in his quarters.

The knock on his door at eleven, announcing Stams's arrival, didn't surprise him. It was the next logical step.

They met in the living room, and Minor stayed quiet, leaving the conversation, whatever it was to be, up to the doctor.

Ellis made himself inconspicuous, but it was apparent to Minor that the young man was debating whether or not to tell Stams about the difficult night.

Stams gave Ellis no chance, anyway. He stood in the center of the floor and said, bluntly, "I've come to put things back under control, Minor. I intend to tell you what's going to take place, and I expect you to accept your role in it without any more accusations or insubordination."

Minor said nothing.

"Our work here is completed. We're ready to announce Minc's existence and send him out to perform the services he was bred to perform. He'll leave tomorrow. Whether you admit it or not, he's ready and fully capable."

"I admit it," Minor said.

Stams didn't acknowledge the statement. He barreled right on, "You, Minor, will take a full month's rest under psychiatric attention. Then, if you're pronounced well enough, I'll put you back to work with a lightened load. From now on, you will concentrate entirely on espionage cases and disaster-forecasting. Minc will handle the international mediations."

Minor had promised himself that he wouldn't, but he was compelled to protest. "You have the work assignments backwards, Doctor. Minc should handle the side jobs and leave the diplomats to me. He has never attempted any of—"

"Are you going to be stubborn about this?" Stams demanded. "You're perfectly aware of what I'm saying, so don't try to fool me. You can grab the thoughts right out of my brain—and who knows how many times you've done it over the years."

Ellis rose. "Now, wait just a *minute,* Dr. Stams."

Stams ignored him. "If you insist on making me say it straight out, Minor, then here it is. We don't really need you

anymore. You're not necessary—PSI man." The last words
were spat out with contempt.

Ellis was out of his chair and beside Minor in three strides,
astounded by Stams's rudeness. "You don't mean that, Dr.
Stams! Not the insult to Counselor Minor's ethics, and not the
last statement, either."

Minor said calmly, "He's serious about every word, Ellis."

"Then why aren't you fighting back?" Ellis was now doing
the demanding.

"Because I knew this would come. Minc has found the way
to push me out. He has Stams by the head, thinking *his*
thoughts, following *his* plans, and probably not even aware of
the fact."

Ellis swung between the two of them, bewildered by things
he had heard nothing about until this moment. "You're just
going to accept it, Counselor?"

"I have no other choice. I gave the warning and asked for
help. No one would listen, so I'm relinquishing all responsibility. To be as blunt as Stams—I'm through! Minc can have
the world. Who can stop him?"

"I won't listen to any more slurs against the boy," Stams
said angrily. "I only want cooperation from you, and a quiet
mouth."

"You'll have both." Minor was resigned to it. "I enjoy making earthquake forecasts, anyway. The only thing remaining to
discover is what hellhole of an asylum Minc has planned for
me."

"Don't dramatize," Stams said. "You're not unbalanced
enough to need an asylum."

"Oh? Hasn't the Clone programmed you that far ahead
yet?" Minor smiled at Stams, then mentally called through the
building, *"Clone! You're letting your puppet run on too long a
leash!"*

"I haven't claimed you're insane, Minor." It was Stams's turn to protest. "Merely exhausted and traumatized. A month of top-level psychiatric counseling will set you right."

Ellis asked honestly, "How can a psychiatrist help a Total-PSI man? It seems to me that the PSI man would be the better psychiatrist."

"Nonsense," Stams huffed. "I personally saved Minor when he collapsed before."

"Did you?" Minor asked. "Or did you simply afford me a place where I could exist as myself?"

Stams had no answer for that, so he cleared his throat and retrieved his former brashness. "Postulating such questions will lead us nowhere. I've said what I came to say. If you want to bid goodbye to your Clone, you'd better be about it, because he'll be leaving here tomorrow. So will you. I appreciate your cooperation—in this part of the affair, anyway."

With Stams's quick exit, Minor found himself facing a shocked and confused Ellis. Personally, Minor was experiencing a strange sense of relief. He had given up responsibility and was ready to wallow in the release of admitting defeat.

But Ellis was too perplexed to keep quiet and let him do it. "I've been cut off from everything all along the way, haven't I? I feel as if I'm in limbo. What has happened, Counselor? And why haven't you confided in me?"

Minor was frank. "Because I thought it would be too dangerous."

Ellis shifted uneasily and abruptly changed the subject. "Can I get you anything? Liquor or coffee?"

"Make it coffee. Resigned to defeat or not, I think I'd better keep a clear head."

The pot was already on a warmer-tray, and as Ellis poured it, concentrating overly hard on the pouring, he confessed in a half-mumble, "I know what you mean by 'dangerous.' And

I'm sorry. When Stams first ordered me to keep a watch on you and report everything you said or did, I refused. But he laid my job on the line, and I figured—probably selfishly—that you'd rather have someone sympathetic playing the spy than to have a stranger."

"It wasn't selfish; it was compassionate. And you were right. You must have gone through some bad moments thinking I might go haywire on you."

"I never mentioned the possibility. I've been worried about you, but not for that reason. Look, is it anything you can talk about? I'm in the dark, and if you'd like to talk it out . . ."

"I don't think so. No."

"Because I'm your 'keeper,' so to speak." Ellis sighed. "You think I'll report what you say. Well, Stams doesn't need to know every detail." Ellis faced Minor square on. "What I'm trying to say is this. I'm still your friend if you want to use me. I'm not dangerous to you. I swear it."

"It wasn't danger to myself I was worried about, Ellis. It was danger to you. But what earthly good would it—"

Ellis interrupted, determined to break down the barriers. "If you have any doubts about me, Counselor, then I'll put myself wide open to you. Probe me. Search me out. I'm giving my consent."

Minor met the blue eyes and shook his head in consternation. For all the young man knew, Minor might be out of control, yet he was willing to give possession of his brain into the suspect hands. And all out of friendship.

"Are you doing it now?" Ellis asked, taking Minor's silent stare to mean the probing was in progress.

"No, and I'm not going to. I trust you, Ellis. I can't say that about anyone else in the world."

"In other words, you're standing alone again. Meeting your Clone didn't help you at all. There is one difference, if you're willing to accept it. Me! Use me, Minor. Tell me what happened with Minc, and what led Stams to turn on you."

"After the statements you've just made, I'd rather get you safely out of here. But"—Minor sighed, rubbing his palm across his forehead—"there won't be a safe place anymore. Not after Minc leaves here tomorrow. I have an awful feeling that his very existence means his success."

"I can't follow what you're saying," Ellis said.

"All right. If you really want to share fear and defeat with me, sit down and I'll tell you everything in detail. I have an idea that you might believe me."

Reciting the story from the first meeting with Minc to the truth about the "nightmares" and Stams's new attitude of pushing him aside brought Minor back to his own starting point. As the story and words petered out, so did he—back into exhaustion and blankness of mind. Because it all began with such great hope and ended with a splintered dream, a shattered man, and a ruined world.

He concluded with, "I made too many mistakes, you see. I had my chance and I lost. Now I'm just relieved that I don't have to care anymore."

"But you do!" Ellis had suffered through it with him, but had arrived at a different conclusion. "That Clone has to be stopped, Minor!"

"I've been through all of that, and it can't be done. Because of his PSI powers. And because it's like asking me to get rid of myself. Unfortunately, we're not so bound together that my suicide would automatically kill him."

"You're not so depressed you'd consider suicide!" Ellis responded sharply. "You have more backbone than that, Minor. I don't care what you've been through or how tired you are; you're too decent to sit there and say, 'I tried and failed, so let the world be damned.'"

"I'd like to say it," Minor admitted. "You put it right on the line, don't you? That's because you're fresh at this. Just beginning."

"Right you are! I'll pick up a gun and go down the hall to destroy that Clone myself, if I have to."

"You wouldn't get within a thousand feet of him."

"I could try! If you're going to crumple into a pile of defeatism—a man who commands faith and trust from the whole world—then it's probably left to me to do! If you can't show me how to destroy him, I'll tackle it any way I can. How do you kill a Total-PSI man? You've as much as said it can't be done with conventional weapons like guns, knives, or surprise attack."

"It can't."

"Of course it can't." Ellis began thinking out loud. "A PSI man operates on the mental level, so it would have to be done mentally. How?"

"If you figure it out, Ellis, let me know. I'll give it a try after my month's stint with the psychiatrist." Minor didn't mean to be sarcastic—not with this particular friend—but he had no stomach for any more trying and failing.

Ellis was red-faced with frustration and spoke freely, his own fear of Minc goading him. "If I dared, Minor, I'd jerk you out of that chair and shake the devil out of you until there was nothing left in you but your conscience. I'm helpless in this situation! You're the only man on this Earth who isn't, so you can't give up on me. Think of the innocents who will die. You have to fight that Clone!"

"With what?" Minor's voice came out loudly, as he felt the spurs of the younger man.

"Your decency, if nothing else. Listen, last night you said that dreams are only for Normals. That when you can see the whole truth, a dream can't exist. I disagree. Minc never was your dream. He's a mistake, not a copy. He didn't live up to you, but you've let him bring you down to his size. Maybe when you looked at the 'whole truth' of that dream, you saw a lie—Minc—and that's what overwhelmed you. Couldn't that be? I say it could."

Minor held his silence, searching the idea through to its end and feeling a stir of energy: touches of it at first; then fingers; then a hard, gripping burst. "I say it could, too," he answered. "Minc isn't my true Clone. Minc isn't the second half of my world. He and I were never destined to share our PSI lives, because he's a grotesque caricature of me. And a demented one. An insane Total-PSI man can't be allowed to survive!"

Minor had half-risen from his chair, energy pouring into him, but he fell back again and cradled his head in his hands.

"What's wrong?" Ellis asked. "You looked as though you'd found a way. What turned you around?"

Minor half-whispered, "The awful realization of what I was saying. The one possibility I hadn't let myself consider." He raised his head and looked up at Ellis with a stunned face. "I have to kill my Clone, don't I? I have to find a way to murder him."

There wasn't time to think about it, and no way to think without warning Minc with every thought he dug up, so Minor took his resolve and strode with it through the carpeted hallways. He had one ace, one terrible method he'd worked out as a boy but of course had never tried. As he sorted back through everything he'd picked up from the first merging, he knew surely that the Clone hadn't considered the idea for himself. So it gave Minor a chance.

Minc would possess the basics of it now, naturally. He had absorbed it in the merging, and the facts would be reinforced at the instant of Minor's attack. But the Clone couldn't be adept at the method, since he'd had no time to mull over the tactics. And he wasn't as strong as his parent-cell. That had already been proved.

Minor sent his PSI call ahead of him. *"Minc! Come to the meeting room. We have things to do before tomorrow."*

"I'm on my way, parent-cell. But you'd better tone down those violent emotions. I don't feel like being threatened."

The Clone had guessed his intent, then. It didn't matter. Minc's insane ego would keep him from taking it seriously. Minor simply held to his resolve, refusing to consider what he was about to do, and praying that it would work. There couldn't be any preamble. He had to pounce, or the Clone would gain too much insight by probing his mind.

He thrust his hand against the door and charged inside. Minc stood in the center of the room, and at the first sight of him Minor halted. He was gazing into his own face again— younger and more vital, but still his own. How could he—?

In that fatal pause, Minc said derisively, "What's the matter, parent-cell? Are you mad at Stams? Are you surprised that even your faithful doctor is finally treating you like the freak you are?"

"Never surprised," Minor answered. "It's your first step at grinding me under your heel. But I didn't come here to—"

"Don't be so melodramatic, parent-cell. I'll never injure you. After all, you have a lot of sentimental value to me. You can stay around, just as long as you keep in your subordinate place and handle only the minor problems. Hear that, Counselor? *Minor* problems? I can use you as a dandy piece of equipment."

Minor stayed where he was, watching this copy of himself pronounce sentiments that were his exact opposite, and in that instant his dream completely died. The Clone was a lie. The Clone was monstrous.

"Shocked, parent-cell?" Minc laughed. "You don't like what I'm saying?"

"No, I don't," Minor growled. "And you'll never say it again."

He flung his mind across the room and powered an entry into the Clone's brain, feeling for new bearings, for areas he'd never tapped before. It was violent and cruel, and Minc staggered backwards under the assault, because this time there was a physical sensation to the probe, a frenzied "hitting" and "manipulating" of the material brain against its skull case, as Minor gouged for the area he wanted and applied pressure, pushing, pinching and crushing the impulse pathways.

Minc opened his mouth to shout an order, but no sound came. His lips moved, but nothing passed them.

"You're voiceless," Minor told him, glorying in his own voice. "I've turned your sound off, Clone. Try to yell for help."

"You cowardly—!" Minc screamed in his PSI voice, clutching at his soundless throat. *"What kind of vicious—?"* He lurched sideways to the nearest chair and caught hold of it, frantic.

Minor fumbled on inside the Clone's brain, buffeting the lobes, searching for what he wanted and creating an inside-out sensation of concussion as his mind tugged and pulled at the pathways, ineptly hunting for areas to match the pictures he'd seen of the brain's structure. He had to hurry! At any second, the Clone could overcome his panic and try to run. He stabbed his PSI power lower into the boy's brain, reaching the cerebellum, the seat of voluntary movements.

At the exact instant Minor found it, Minc heaved himself up to get away. But he stopped in his tracks, bound to the floor by legs that wouldn't answer the command of a suppressed "action center." Only his eyes were left alive, riveted blackly on Minor's, wide and wild with fear.

In spite of himself, Minor couldn't bear that look, and said, "It will be over soon. If you'll . . ."

"You're trying to kill me!"

"God forgive me, yes," Minor said, and guilt erupted out of him, coated with compassion.

Minc's eyes changed, not responding to the compassion, but slitting and shooting darts of energy. *"You can't, Minor. It can only end with both of us dead. What you can do, I can do. Did you forget that?"*

"I didn't."

"And you want to die?"

"Not really. But if it's the only safe answer for the world, then that's the way it is. Prototype and copy—both gone."

"No more freaks? I told you before, I'm not a freak!" Minc's eyes were ablaze. *"Maybe you are insane, but I'm not, and I won't die! Not this way. Are you prepared to watch me struggle? Look at me! I'm you. You have to know that. We waited so long to be together, and now . . . Father! Fathers don't kill their own sons!"* But his eyes never lost their cunning.

"Don't do this," Minor pleaded.

"But what have I done wrong? I've only made the best of a terrible, lonely—"

"You're sly, Minc, and I won't hear it. Not when you play so openly on what you know are my weaknesses. I have to get on with this. I intended it to be quick, but you're making it tor—" His voice quit in mid-word. He tried to utter "torture" again, but nothing came out.

"You didn't even feel me doing it!" Minc laughed. *"I'm better at it than you are because you've already shown me where*

to hit. Now see how it feels to be rooted to one spot, parent-cell!"

Minor felt the jolt this time and found that his legs wouldn't respond. He stood there, balanced but immobile. The Clone was right! He could work faster, because Minor led the way. Yet that still left Minor in command, one step ahead.

"A moment ago you were crying 'Father,'" Minor cursed. *"All right, Clone, the lines are drawn and the guilt is gone. We go from here."*

He set to work with new intensity, staring back at the eyes that were mirroring him, feeling Minc's heavy fist compressing his own brain as they turned each other's body functions off one at a time.

Hearing went next, but they could still damn each other with PSI. Then a great sleepiness overcame Minor as Minc attacked some part of the brain Minor had sidestepped in the Clone as he searched only for the vital center. He fought the sleepiness, driving on. He had to beat the Clone to the medulla —the heart.

Suddenly Minc was dim before him. Two black circles appeared on his face; he turned a strange tint of green and blanked out. Minor was blind! Mute, deaf, immobile and blind.

No matter, he told himself. Let the boy keep his vision. His heart was more important.

With his own body damping down, sense by sense and section by section, he plodded his PSI way through the maze of nerves and impulses, incredibly clumsy, and damning himself for his clumsiness. He should have been able to attack the area that controlled the heartbeat immediately, but as his unschooled "fingers" touched a new center and delivered a crushing blow, he felt a thump reverberate through the floor, and

Minc shrieked, *"You've paralyzed me! I've fallen! Let me go, Minor!"*

Before the scream died away, Minor himself was falling, buckling at the knees and crumpling against the carpet. He paid no attention. Doggedly probing for the center he wanted, he was guided either by a descriptive curse from Minc to tell him what he had already done, or by Minc's battling duplication of it in Minor's own body to demonstrate it.

Lying there, forcing himself to stay awake and focus his power, Minor became aware that there were longer intervals between his inhalations and exhalations. The Clone had slowed his breathing! If Minc halted his lungs entirely, it would be as deadly as stopping his heart. And Minc would win.

Trying not to count the intervals between breaths—always longer—or heed the dizziness and chest tightness, he pressed on inside the Clone's brain, picking up the lung-stopping procedure from Minc, and setting off the same reaction in the Clone. Minor wanted to gasp, but his chest wouldn't respond with a gasp. His mind was fuzzy for lack of oxygen, and all he could do was pray that his greater strength would let him endure longer than the Clone.

He knew that what breaths he did take must be hoarse and rattling, announcing death. Blessedly, he couldn't hear them. Minc was hearing his, but there was no time to take pity and stop the boy's auditory sense. Minor had to strike the heart. And now!

"I'm suffocating!" Minc cried out. *"Please, Minor! Counselor! Don't do this! I can see you lying there—and you're alive—so you don't have to leave me like this. Let me go. Please!"*

Minor didn't respond.

"Have it your way, then." Minc was nearly sobbing, not from fear or pleading, but with malevolent fury. *"I'm younger,*

and I'm not worn out like you are. I can win just by outlasting you. Die, Minor-parent-cell. There never was a place for you in the world, and there certainly isn't one in mine!"

With that last vicious curse bursting in his mind, Minor touched home. The Clone's mental cry of pain told him that the boy's heart was affected, contracting spasmodically, burbling out the last blood it would ever course through his body. It was almost done.

Minc's PSI gasps went on and on, growing weaker until they ceased, but Minor held to the pressure, fighting to keep conscious, because the Clone's mind was still alive and still depressing Minor's lungs.

Four minutes. Could he make it through four more minutes? Yes! He realized with a surge that would have jerked his body if it had been able to move. Even if his lungs stopped entirely, he would also have the added minutes of diminishing brain life. He'd be dead when they found him. But so would his Clone.

He held on, releasing the pressure he had been applying to other areas of the Clone's brain to concentrate it all on the heart. It was hard enough, and constantly harder, to do even that much. He was heading into blackness himself. Death was close, and he knew it, but he held on.

With a sensation of "absence," he was aware that he had ceased to breathe. The sleepiness became giant-sized. He had nothing left of strength-to-fight or stamina-to-resist.

This was how the dream ended then. How eighteen years concluded. Both of them dead together. So be it.

Quietly—like a faint and silent gasp—the Clone's mind turned off. All that was left to Minor's weak probes was emptiness.

Minc was dead. The other half of his world didn't exist. But neither did *his* half, not when it was lungless. He lay there and gave himself over to sleep.

"No one's trying to stall you, Stams," Ellis said. "The doctor will be through in a minute, and then you can—"

"The doctor is through right now." Dr. Ramison came out of the bedroom.

"And?" Stams demanded. "Can Bates and I finally see him? We've waited two days already, and you originally said one."

Ramison shrugged. "The extra time was Minor's choice. My guess is that he wanted to postpone your jumping on him until he felt up to full capacity."

"And he is now?" Bates asked.

"He'll be able to take anything you throw. But my suggestion is to keep yourselves to darts and away from spears. After all, knowing what he's capable of doing . . ." Ramison let the sentence hang and left the room, on his way back to the medical clinic inside the building.

Stams was put slightly off balance by the statement, but hid it immediately as Minor himself came out of the bedroom. "You don't look as bad as I expected," Stams told Minor, then elevated himself again by adding, "and definitely not as bad as you should."

"I'm fine, thanks to Ellis," Minor answered. "He deserves a bonus or something, Stams. He was sure that he was walking to his own death, but he charged into that room anyway, in time to yell for help and then keep me alive with his own life's breath."

Ellis made light of his action. "I was the only one who knew what you were doing, and you were gone so long. I had to check on you."

"You saved my life," Minor stated flatly.

"But not the boy's," Stams said. "That's what I meant before, Minor, that you don't look as bad as a killer should."

"I see," Minor answered with a wry smile. "Ellis saved me just so I can be tried for murder. And executed?" He kept the smile on his face, directed at Stams.

His "controller" quickly backed down. "No—I mean—of course not. Although you should be. Murder is murder, Counselor."

"And that precious boy," Bates moaned. "When we heard what you'd done, we couldn't believe it. I still can't. I feel as though I'd lost part of my family. If the world ever finds out what it has lost . . ." He shook his head, true disappointment and grief overriding his anger.

"Well, here I stand." Minor still smiled, determined to play at least some of this Minc's way and keep power over his own fate for a change. "Which one of you wants to aim the gun?"

"Now you're mocking us," Stams protested. "You know full well that we can't take any reprisals against you. You're too valuable to the world. But what happened to you, Minor, to let you do a vicious thing like that?"

"I finally grew up, Stams. I found out that if a man is alone, then he's alone—physically, mentally, or in whatever he values as truth. I knew that Clone. No one else would believe what I said about him, and no one else could have handled him anyway, so it was left to me. I simply stood my ground and did it.

"From now on, there will be no more adolescent dreams for me. I am what I am. The Clone taught me that much. I'm not a freak, or even a misfit. I'm a special human being. An advanced human being, with the right to control my own life. And," he added deliberately, "with the ability to do it against anyone who stands in my way."

Bates raised his breathless voice, afraid again. "You murdered my Minc with your PSI power? Only with that?"

"Exactly. Did you find a mark on him?"

"Not one," Bates said. "The autopsy showed heart attack."

"Induced heart attack," Minor stated, and added slyly, "You see, gentlemen, I *am* powerful. More than I've ever admitted. I kept too much of myself secret before, and maybe that's why you wouldn't believe me when I told you the Clone could ruin the world. But I'm not hiding any longer."

Stams stared at him, nervous, but willing to brazen it out. "Are you trying to intimidate us, Minor? If you are, then forget it, because as far as I'm concerned, it's work as usual. There's nothing we can do about a dead Clone, so we're left with you. Therefore, you have to continue in your role as PSI Counselor."

"I'm perfectly willing, Stams. Does that surprise you? I'll even go you one better. I also intend to keep to my own principles about using PSI without consent. The Clone didn't change me that much. What I *do* demand is more respect from you, or anyone who comes after you. I want no more threats of collapse, and no more manipulating. I'll do the work because I want to do it, not because I'm given orders."

Stams remained silent, considering the alternatives, then said, "Very well, those conditions are granted. To be truthful, I don't want to stay on with you, anyway. But there's one order you'll have to follow. Directly upon leaving here, you're to go to the Biological Science Center to undergo cloning again."

"No."

"You have no choice."

"I always have a choice—now. I'm willing to continue my work for the sake of the planet and its people, but I'll do it on a voluntary basis and not as a piece of machinery. I'm not a mere lie-detector or pre-seismograph. That's what the Clone wanted of me. I wouldn't do it for him, and I won't do it for you. One of me is enough for the world. It might happen that if everyone realizes I'm mortal, they'll find a way to settle their squabbling once and for all so they can survive without me."

"I don't agree," Stams insisted. "We need your talents. And as I said, you can be forced into the cloning."

"How?" Minor smiled again, keeping his posture of reined-in threat.

"He can't be forced, Dr. Stams," Bates said quickly. "Don't antagonize him, for heaven's sake. His way is best. I certainly don't want to raise any more of his Clones. Not when I know what they can do."

"There isn't a way to force you, is there?" Stams finally admitted. "Then we're stymied."

"No, you aren't," Ellis spoke up. "Counselor Minor can't be forced, but he can be asked."

"Someone else will have to do the asking." Stams clamped his jaw tight. "I don't beg favors from killers." He latched his eyes onto Minor and drew a great breath, as though he were wary of what he intended to say but would say it anyway. "If nothing else, Minor, I can take credit for unmasking you. Now that you've dropped your pretenses, you stand clear as what I knew you to be all along. Don't think you fooled me. I refuse to accept any further responsibility for your behavior. Someone else can shoulder you from this point on. I've endured all that one man should be asked to endure."

Bates interrupted him. "Are you sure you should be saying this?"

"Just be quiet and come along, Bates," Stams commanded. "We'll leave him to a higher authority."

Bates followed him out willingly, and Minor and Ellis were left alone.

"That takes two more devils off my tail," Minor said, chuckling.

"But not this one." Ellis pointed to his own chest. "I'm going to ask you to agree to the cloning. For your own sake. You've changed a lot, yes—in confidence and awareness of your own worth. But think ahead a little. That special dream you waited for and wanted so much—you still haven't realized it. You haven't even come close. You may need it in the future as much as you did in the past."

Minor rested his dark eyes gently on the blue ones that had turned so quickly into the friendliest, most trustworthy pair on Earth. "Since we've sworn to be open with each other from now on, Ellis, I have a confession to make. Although I'll lay odds you already know. What I did to my Clone is something I'll never be able to accept or forget. I ache with it now, and I always will. As for the dream, and the hope of another 'like' human being to share my life, I thought it died on the floor of that room. It didn't."

Ellis smiled. "Thank God. I couldn't believe you'd really turned into arrogant ice."

"That little scene was simply petty revenge against Stams. Not that I didn't mean what I said about having free will from now on, because I intend to demand it."

"But you will agree to the cloning?"

"Of course. There was too much in Minc that I wanted to love. I have to try again. Actually, I considered requesting it, and I've been working out plans for the last two days."

"What kind of plans? A cloning is a cloning."

"Not one cloning, Ellis. Twenty! With these stipulations: first, they are to grow up together, so they can be spared the loneliness and the isolation; and second, I'll insist on free access to them so I can tutor their PSI powers and, even more important, so I can implant a good, sensitive conscience in each one of them. No boy will ever have to die again because some Normal bungles his training. If anyone tries to hide them away from me, I'll shake down the world."

"And you could do it," Ellis said, with a touch of pride and devilment. He still wasn't afraid of the man he had made his friend.

Minor shook his head and laughed softly. "You see? I told you I might populate the world with myself. How about that?"

LOVE
ROGO

Jeffrey A. Carver

Why I sensed that Rogo would enjoy a walk on the Sea Cliff Terrace I don't honestly know, but I had the afternoon off and wanted to give my new friend a treat. Even then he seemed to be "our" B-mot, though we had hardly had him long enough to decide whether we wanted to keep him. He had looked so helpless sitting at our door, and he was such a thoroughly pleasant fellow, and Janice liked his name so much—I couldn't foresee that either of us would ever want to send him away.

Too bad, that.

Rogo looked more or less like a dog most of the time—although as I watched him galumphing with me along the pedestrifare he seemed more to resemble an oversized bumper-pillow with four feet and two eyes. At other times he looked like a brown earless bunny, or a down-covered basset hound with small pointed ears where the big flappers should have been. B-mots change in their appearance from time to time, which is awfully disconcerting, and until I adjusted to it I was forever thinking my eyes were trying to be funny.

Rogo charged on down through the public doors and sat eagerly waiting, his head twitching in the breeze. There were relatively few people about, and it looked to be a fine day outside the plexopolis. I hurried to join him, glad to smell the fresh salt air after two weeks indoors. "Feels good, eh, Rogo?" I luxuriated in the air from the sea; my cheeks livened at the cool, washing, shoreward breeze. Rogo perked his ears and twisted his head around with a doglike grin. We crossed the broad Terrace to get to the sea-railing, Rogo romping ahead of me and planting himself blissfully at the rail, facing seaward. As I caught up with him, he barked, without bothering to look around. His "bark" was more of a sigh, like air crying from a balloon whistle, pitched high and sliding down to a melancholy moan.

"Yeah, that's nice, Rog'; you're absolutely right." The view was superb: the ocean splayed out in lines and streaks from the Terrace-topped cliff, breakers and distant whitecaps glittered in the afternoon sun, and from somewhere at the base of the cliff the cascade and crumple of water like repeating landslides kicked spray almost high enough to wet the Terrace. I leaned out over the railing, eyes half closed, gathering a hint of salty mist in my nostrils, against my face. Seen through slitted eyes, the sky itself was a blue-gray cotton sea, a shifting matrix of interloping currents of fluid and light and vertiginous depth. There was a sense of saturation in the sight, sharpened to a clear crystal by voices in the air, voices of walkers, loungers, lovers, arguers—and, over all, the lumber and hiss of the sea.

Sitting just close enough to hug my leg, Rogo was breathing with a soft, repeated sigh, a sound that was something between a purr and a contented hum. I liked his presence; he did not seem at all like a stranger. "Rogo, boy," I said, "I think we're going to keep you." And I swear he understood. He craned his ruffed neck and looked up at me with his small mouth partly open and his eyes filled with solemn and total devotion. Touched by this display, I batted him gently on the nose.

Too soon we had to start home for supper, and that meant a good four-section, three-level hike into the plexopolis, the enclosed city which the Terrace bordered like some giant's flowing mantel. As usual, my timing was precisely wrong; I have a knack for stumbling into the worst rushes on the pedestrifares. We were pushed and harried and delayed all the way to the Clarendon Level, and at times I had to swing my arms like a turnstyle just to keep mindless pedestrians from trampling Rogo. But through an hour of curses and elbows and body odor I not only kept my temper, I kept my good humor— and that was astonishing. I saw boredom, impatience, vicious ugliness on tired and hungry faces, but somehow it keyed my senses, made me brightly aware that there was *life* around me; and I found that the more turmoil I saw, the more alert I became. Rogo woofed and grinned whenever some moron stumbled over one of us, and while that may not seem like much, it kept me jolly, kept me happy, and kept the whole ridiculous business somehow in perspective, so that I could absorb the brutal jostling and dish it right back, all without losing an ounce of good spirits. I have no idea how he did it. I guess it was just his crazy B-mot manner.

I felt so good when we got home, I almost raped Janice before she could say hello.

"Aren't we frisky today!" she yelped in surprise, escaping from my clutches like a veteran. "What's got you so friendly?" She was starting to laugh.

That, I thought, was unnecessary. She looked terribly appealing in her clingy saffron houserobe—which was curious, since I had told her any number of times that I didn't like that robe. "Dunno," I said over my shoulder, going into the bathroom. When I came out again, I peered into the microcook to see whether anything was cooking—nothing was—and said, "We're keeping Rogo, okay?"

"Huh?"

"He's great company, and—look at him—we can't turn him in to the Commissioner. Who knows where he'd wind up? He trusts us—look at that." She turned and looked. Rogo was sitting respectfully by the door, as if waiting for us to finish the discussion and cast our votes, thumbs up or thumbs down. His fur was camel-brown at the moment and exceedingly fluffed, and he looked at us with dark, gumdrop eyes, ready to leave at once if that was what we wanted.

"We really don't have room, you know, Lackey dear."

"How much room can he take?"

"Well, I don't know—we'd have to get a permit." Her eyebrows were crunched together very thoughtfully.

"So we'll get one tomorrow. What do you say?" I took her by the shoulders and smiled, disarmingly, I hoped.

"Hmm. Okay." She grinned and kissed me suddenly. The sneak—she had been sold all along; she had just wanted to make me work for it.

"Rogo, you're in!" I shouted, hugging Janice fiercely. Rogo allowed himself a woof-sigh and settled down for a nap in his new home. Janice and I settled in for our own kind of celebration.

The night improved as it went along. While we didn't get around to supper until quite late, we enjoyed each other more that night than we had in ages. It was funny, because we had been snipping at each other for months, and suddenly that was all behind us. It was as if all those months had been a long pause, as if we had been holding our breath, and now we were free to tumble even more desperately into love than before. Rogo lay serenely near the foot of our bed while we made love, and his occasional wistful sighs filled our moments of silence nicely, making it all seem that much more right. The night fled quickly as we slept in tired, tangled peacefulness.

Though I felt springy and spry in the morning, I wanted to call in sick at work. But Janice talked me out of it, saying that she had to go to school anyway. So I went to the office and to my astonishment was afflicted by a sudden rush of interest in my work. Now, a job shuffling government personnel forms is not a likely target for enthusiasm, but I found myself actually reading documents I had handled for years, and suddenly I was marveling at the intricate nonsense that government paperwork entails. Employment histories, regional residency histories, mating histories, security ratings . . . I not only worked my full five hours; I stayed a half hour overtime.

When Janice got home from her art classes, we went down and registered Rogo at the Pet Commissioner's office:

CERTIFICATE OF REGISTRY OF RESIDENTIAL PET

Description of pet: B-mot. Name of pet: Rogo
Circumstances of acquisition: He acquired us (stray).
Veterinary clearance documentation: To be obtained.
Name of owner(s): John Lackland; Janice Lieberkind.
If joint ownership, length of prior cohabitation: 1½ years.
Residence of owner(s): 924A-K Third Floor Clarendon Level; same.
Occupation(s) of owner(s): G-11b Reg. Gov. Person. Clerk; Student.
Soc. Sec. No. owner(s): 3-647-55-6915, 3-654-82-9164.
Permit number, pet (to be assigned by Office of Commissioner): Bmt-34895AK.

. . . and so on and on; there was lots more of the same sort of thing. Three pages' worth, not counting duplicates, and I examined it all with great care and delight. Then, once he was official, we took old Bmt-34895AK to the nearest vet, who pronounced him fit and healthy. This was basically a formality, since B-mots are considered immune to terrestrial diseases anyway, but we needed the clearance note for the Pet Commissioner. By the time we were finished with all the tape-running, it was too late to do anything recreational that day, so we went home and hatched a plot for the following day.

I'd had a premonition that my new-found enthusiasm for work was likely to wear thin rather quickly, so instead of putting it to the test, I shuffled some papers bearing my own name and secured myself a week's advance vacation, beginning immediately. Janice, meanwhile, arranged for someone to cover for her in class. It was an outrageous thing for us to do, and we knew we'd pay for it later, but we were in the crazy high of having a good time for ourselves, and we just said, What the hell? So we made our excuses and ran, with Rogo.

We headed up the coast by train, several hundred kilometers north and a hundred or so inland, to Mount Adrexica—the man-made mountain which neither Janice nor I (nor, presumably, Rogo) had ever seen. It was an impressive edifice, appearing to be a hybrid between a real mountain and some of the old amusement park varieties; according to the guide literature it had been built largely out of industrial glassy slag and clinkers—urban refuse from an entire region—and sealed (they sounded as if they were joking) with Lake Erie dredge spoil. The basic lumpy mountain was then cut and shaped with fusors and carefully triggered landslides, filled, planted, landscaped, and finally frosted with snow and even a small glacier near the summit.

After checking into the Winterside Lodge, we spent the better part of the afternoon just gawking at the mountain from the various overlooks, finding it utterly entrancing: sleek false-winter snow capping the upper slopes and curling down and around the lower ones, here sweeping along a smooth-carved ski run, there dropping from an overhang down an ice-ornamented precipice. Skiers swam like dots and clusters down the wrinkles and ridges of the mountain's skin, then zipped out at the bottom onto a great wide apron of fresh powder. No ski lift was visible, just skiers disappearing into the mouth of the underground elevator like bowling balls into a hidden return. Janice was interested in the people rambling in and out of the chalet, brightly plumed and muffled folk with skis under their arms, a few of them with the longer and slower old-style skis, and everyone chattering and laughing, as if the crisp bright aura of the mountain had exorcised all spirits but glittering enthusiasm.

After a while, we hurried down from the promenade ourselves and went outside onto the snow. Rogo at first poked nervously at the edge of the icy, powdery stuff and sat himself down just clear of it, sighing and grinning wolfishly; but finally, with a lot of whistling and foolish giggling, we coaxed him out into the snow and got him romping like an excited puppy, bouncing and digging and coming up with snootfuls of snow. Being lowslung, he was never quite able to lift himself clear of the white stuff, so he looked as though he were swimming or belly-crawling, when he was actually just trying to walk. His fur rippled in the air like satin ruffles, gradually turning a pale buff, and it probably would have turned as white as a seal cub's coat if we'd stayed out long enough. When he focused his jet-black eyes on us to announce that he was getting cold, we raced with him back to the patio and the fireplace warmth of the chalet.

Around on the Summerside of Adrexica was the Gladepool, and that was where we headed for next. It sat beneath straight, tall snow-topped cliffs which split outward at the mountain's foot to shoulder a vale lush with vegetation, with the crystalline blue pool basin at its lower end. The air was heated, moist, and ripe with a flowery sweetness and the scent of ferns. We started our exploration with a stroll through a wide grove between the Summerside Chalet and the pool.

Here the only bit of unpleasantness marred a near-perfect day.

A tired-looking man stumbled toward us from somewhere off in the grove; he was leading a gray B-mot, not quite so large as Rogo, and he was drunk. Before he was even close, we smelled the Erythraean gin. "Hey, there!" he shouted—to whom, we didn't know. Janice urged me ahead, hoping to avoid him, but the man called out again, and this time it was clear he was addressing us. He walked up, swaying unpleasantly close to my face. "That beast of yours," he said, staring at me with a glazed, drunken intensity, "that thing is going to be a troublemaker; look at 'im."

I looked at Rogo, standing docilely. I looked at the man. "What?" I said.

"Yah, you say that. Here, now, keep him away from my Ricky." Rogo had noticed the other B-mot, and the two animals were touching noses but showing no great excitement. The man toed Rogo, who backed away hastily, looking insulted. If he had hurt Rogo, I would have slugged him. "Yah, you stay away from my Ricky," he grumbled. He looked around dazedly, suddenly ignoring us. He turned, coughed hoarsely, and croaked, "Place sure isn't all it's billed to be, is it?" Then laughed—an ugly, drunken laugh.

My good mood was gone, and I was becoming angry. What right, for god sakes, did this pitiful fool have to spoil our day?

"Listen," I said, straining to keep my voice level, "there are a thousand other places you can go if you don't like it here." Janice was harrumphing, plucking at my arm, but now that this ass had bothered us, I was going to make it clear to him that I didn't like it at all.

"Sure, sure," he said blandly. "You and the woman getting a real charge out of all this, huh?" He chuckled obscenely, leered at Janice, looked back at me, and turned away.

"Listen, you—" I started, raising my fists, but Janice had a firm grip on me now. The epitome of calm. She caught my eye and shook her head. She knew damned well I had no tact when insulted, nor did I have intimidating bulk or the blessing of an agile tongue. In any case, the man was walking away with his Ricky; we had been forgotten. "Let's go, Rog'," I growled, and let Janice pick a new heading through the woods.

I was burning, my pride and my dignity offended, but I rather relished the feeling—it was the first genuine anger I had felt in months, and it was a purging anger; not boredom or frustration, but good honest malice. I gripped Janice's hand tightly as we walked, smelling the wood-green smells of the grove, feeling the spring of fallen pine needles under my feet, and living my anger to its fullest in the rushing world sealed in my mind—until the anger had burned itself pure and my good humor returned. The transformation was as cleanly perceptible as the rush of a clear liquor's vapors to my skull. We left the woods and walked at the edge of the pool basin and sat in the grass under a warming sun. Janice smiled at me, glad to see me happy again; the incident seemed not to have affected her at all. I touched her nose with a finger, stroked the front strands of her hair. When Rogo poked his head between ours to get his share of the affection, I roughed him up vigorously, and he sighed in perfect contentedness.

"We'll remember this," Janice said later, walking with her hand in mine around the pool. The water was utterly flat, a clear blue in the midst of the verdant leaves. The pool was fed from beneath, the basin an asymmetric funnel, darkening in the middle to its indiscernible source. "Mm-hm," I answered. Janice talked that way when she was feeling very close, very gentle, very much in love—and that was how I always answered.

Rogo lurched and nipped at the pool's bank, and we laughed quietly as we watched the sun breaking up behind the trees as it sank, and watched each other and were as happy as we would ever be in our lives.

No one seems to know just how the B-mots acquired their peculiar name. No doubt I have failed to ask the proper individuals. All I know is that they were brought here a few years back by the visitors from Betelgeuse—those gangling fellows who toured Earth with all the fanfare and spotlights. They brought along some of their pets, which after the official welcomings they displayed enclosed in strange little spheres for all the scientists and media people to see and record. They had a regular sampler of Betelian native stock, including plants and fishes and land animals. Under scientific supervision, some of these were released into Earth-type environments; a few died, but most were adaptable to Earth and appeared quite harmless. This was all very enlightening scientifically, no doubt, but the scientists could hardly have predicted the spectacular popularity of one animal, the B-mot, for which even one-time viewers developed a quick and unshakable adoration. The B-mots were the new darlings, and they seemed to love people as much as people loved them. Eventually the powers that be decided that it was all right to turn them loose, and the Betelians happily provided several hundred for distribution.

The B-mots bred like crazy, and soon it was possible for nearly everyone to have one. According to the Betelians, they would reproduce as long as they were happy, but not to excess —they would never breed in burdensome numbers. It seemed to be true; at least, I had never heard of anyone's wanting to wish them away. The Betelians themselves, I believe, went home. Don't quote me on that—some of them may still be around somewhere.

To Janice and me, Rogo was an all-new experience, and we learned as we went along. For a time, it seemed too easy—he ate little and kept himself clean—and we were lulled into believing that the cost of owning him would be no greater. He occupied a great deal of our attention, though, mainly just by being lovable, and we thought this a blessing. He was always jolly, or, if one of us was angry or depressed, sympathetic—the perfect companion.

Janice usually got home before I did and would often take Rogo out for some exercise and play—which was fine with me, until I began coming home to a place that was empty until suppertime. Eventually I chided her gently about this, and she blushed and promised never to let it happen again. "But," she said wryly, "who greets Rogo so effusively that half the time he forgets to say Hi to his beloved roommate, hmm?" Well, she had a point there. I grinned sheepishly and promised, et cetera, and we were both happy again, at least for a while.

My work started to get me down, though, mainly because of my boss. Mrs. Curtzen is a vicious old lady at heart, I believe, and when she chose to interrupt my peaceful reverie with her grating voice next to my ear, I would virtually shrivel on the spot. "You didn't have enough time on your vacation, Mr. Lackland?" would come the singsong-query nagging. A scowl, a shrug, and then back to looking as though I were working. Ah, but the reverie! Ever since the beginning of our trip, I had felt a glow in my fingertips, a sharpening of my senses. I was filled with marvelous conceptions of space, colors, smells, temperature rhythms, sound flows. Strange perceptions constantly at my notice. From my seat at work I had a perfect view of the lines, the depth of the office, the play of light on the curves of the desks and chairs. I listened to the heartbeat in my head, and noticed little twinges and tickles in my nervous system—signals, I suppose, of discharges, systems clearing the boards or recharging for the next round. Pleasant, intriguing—but I wasn't getting much work done. "Mr. Lackland, shall I call the supervisor and tell him you're not happy with your work?" Damn woman. I'd shake my head, dive energetically into my work.

When I wasn't lost in a symphony of senses, I was lost in thought, wondering why not; what was wrong with me?

I told Janice, and she gave me a Well, what can you expect? look and said, tugging at a piece of yarn on a tapestry puzzle she was making, "You ought to start thinking more like a robot when you're at work. Save some of that creative energy for me. You've been slipping a bit lately, you know."

Was that the best she could do? I had to act like a robot; did I have to think like one, too? Hey, wait a minute! "Who's been slipping? Me?" She slid one lip up over the other, half-smiled, shrugged. She would say no more, but she watched me as I walked around for a while, frowning and wondering.

We had gotten into the habit in the evenings of taking Rogo for walks in Clarendon Park, an indoor arboretum with some flowers and trees and a small aviary, all housed under a geodesic dome at the edge of Clarendon Level. It was a convenient place to let Rogo run. Out the right side of the dome, one could see, in staggered fashion downward, the lighted domes of Berkeley and Arlington parks, while above and to the left were the stepping-slab undersides of the upper-level parks, all dark and shadowy. The real attraction, though, was the Clarendon garden itself. Rogo liked to poke around the shrubbery; he snuffed his way curiously, with almost feline delicacy, rarely touching anything, even with his nose. Janice and I simply enjoyed the view and the flowers, and watched Rogo with his insatiable interest. It struck me as a curious thing that he was an alien from another world, because to us he was just someone with whom we shared our lives.

I was almost afraid to say it, but finally one night I remarked to Janice that I was getting a little tired of the park. Actually, I thought I was just in a soul-slump at the time, because I hadn't been enjoying much of anything lately. "Maybe it's the dog shit," she said dryly. I chuckled and dropped the subject, but I wondered what had prompted such a nasty remark. That was a long-standing annoyance to her, but she had been carefully keeping it to herself for harmony's sake. Well, one would have had to suppose that there was B-mot shit involved, too, although B-mots tend to be more discreet than dogs.

More deeply disturbing was her behavior later that night, when she became coldly cranky for no reason I could fathom. Rogo and I had worked up a game involving our polywater bed, which he loved bouncing around on, especially when it was rolling like surf. We played a sort of keep-away, with me jouncing the mattress energetically while Rogo fumbled with a Floppo-Ball too big for him to hold in his jaws which lurched and bounced crazily—and that was what Rogo did, also, romping and stumbling, and somehow always turning on his nose. B-mots do not normally turn on their noses. Rogo thought it great fun, and he could have gone on long after I tired.

I thought Janice was angry because she felt neglected. But when I apologized, she scowled and punched another video cassette into her study-deck. "If you're that crazy about him, go back and play," she muttered sullenly.

"Hey!" I went around in front of her so she would look at me. "Don't you like him, too?" Of course I knew she did; something else was wrong.

"Sure. I'll get in my hour another time." She ignored me, pretending to study. I was amazed; I couldn't believe she was seriously jealous of Rogo.

Dumbly I went back to sit beside Rogo. I wondered what was going on, and why I wasn't doing anything about it. I should have tried to get her to talk, but for a long time I didn't; I was hurt, and I just didn't want to. Finally, Janice accused me of not caring very much. "I care," I said defensively. But she didn't want to believe me, and she wouldn't listen. "Janice, talk to me now—don't just be mad."

Arched eyebrows. Back to her studying.

I sensed that jealousy was not the problem. It was something else—chemistry, brain waves, something. Okay, every couple has occasional bad nights. We'd been lucky to have had so few.

Before we went to bed, she said, "I'm sorry, Lackey. I'm not mad at you or Rogo. I'm mad at myself."

Which helped not at all. Rogo knew what was going wrong —oh yes—but by the time I understood, my world was far too far gone.

Shortly thereafter my work began to improve, in a manner of speaking. I was growing numb to it and was therefore less distracted, which kept Mrs. Curtzen off my back. In point of fact, I was growing numb to quite a lot of things. My walk to the office took me through a variety of neighborhoods, past noisy and interesting shops on Berkeley Level, but I found myself arriving at work or at home with hardly any impression in my mind of what the walk had been like. It was not that I was failing to pay attention; I saw the shops, the signs, the displays, the milling people, but none of it was sinking in; none of it mattered; none of it seemed worth remembering.

I was frightened, in the way one might fear a potentially serious and protracted illness. I had always prided myself on my appreciation of things around me. Perhaps it was just the weather outside, the season, the ions in the air. It was temporary; things would return to normal, I thought. But somewhere within me I suspected otherwise.

Then Janice confessed to me that she had been skipping her classes for the past two weeks. I was surprised; I didn't know what to say. "What have you been doing?" I asked.

"Walking," she said, "sitting at home, going out. Sometimes I take Rogo." She tried to smile, but the smile was an impoverished effort, flickering on her lips like a futilely struggling candle flame.

I started to tell her what she was risking by skipping school, but she stopped me immediately. Yes, yes, she said; but she couldn't concentrate, she was bored. "Oh." I had thought she liked her classes. "What's wrong, anyway?"

She looked at me very strangely for a long minute, as if she thought I knew very well what was wrong. She had not reckoned with my obtuseness, however. "My paintings: they're dull, gray, worse than nothing at all." She said it very emphatically, very dejectedly. Then she walked out into the kitchen and left me standing with a strange tight pressure across my chest, in a room full of emptiness, as if the air had exploded out of the room. I sat and stared into the distance of a blank blue wall and wondered how it was that everything I prized was tumbling, going to gray, turning flat; I was hardly aware that Rogo was beside me, absorbing the strokes of my hand on his fur with muffled, healthy little sighs. When he moaned and caught my attention, I realized that my hand was on his ruffed neck, and I jerked it back as if bitten; and I wondered, Now, why did I do that?

Later, I found Janice walking in a slow dance around Rogo, studying him as if he were a statuette for sale in a gallery. She stooped, touched his middle with her fingertips, looked exasperated and thoughtful. Rogo looked oblivious. "Measuring him for a dress or for the cooker?" I asked her.

"Mmm," she said, paying no attention.

"How's that again?" She still ignored me, so I tapped her on the arm.

She looked up, startled. "Hi," she grunted. "I was just thinking that this fellow is getting a bit big. And I wondered why."

"Feeding him too much." We fed him hardly anything.

"Uh-huh. John, how sure are we that Rogo's a guy?"

"The vet said so."

"Well, can little boy B-mots get pregnant?" She knelt beside him, stroking his flanks gently.

"Well, why don't we ask the vet? Never thought about it, myself." The idea was mildly disturbing, but I figured that taking him back to the medicine man would give us something to do.

We did, and he was. Pregnant. According to the vet, he still was a he, so we learned something else that day: B-mots are androgynous, or something along those lines. We did not press for a fuller explanation, because frankly we were too shocked at the thought of having a prospective mother on our hands. Rogo took the news calmly, silently.

On the way home Janice told me she didn't know whether she wanted to keep him. Our nice male pet was going to fill the living room with babies—that was a very *alien* thing to do, she said. And there was something else about Rogo that both-

ered her, but she chickened out of saying it, and that was as
close as we came to bringing our growing suspicions into the
open. (Now, why were we afraid? Was it some extraordinary
embarrassment, or was it just part of his power over us, his
charm that we were afraid to question or insult? Or were we
merely stupid?) Janice kept me awake half the night, staring at
me in the gloom from her side of the bed. "We can't just throw
the poor guy out," I insisted logically. "Besides, you used to
like him too."

"I *do* like him; he's adorable! But he's got me suspicious.
What do we really know about him?" That he was turning us
into glassy-eyed nervous wrecks? That was what I thought, but
I didn't say it. Janice turned her back to me, making it clear
that she considered the situation hopeless. Before she went to
sleep I reminded her that we had a few weeks yet to decide before Rogo's babies were due.

I hadn't forgotten that Rogo was no Earthling. But only
now did it occur to me to wonder why he had left his last
owner . . . or why he had been thrown out. Could he have
been pregnant that long ago? Had his previous owner reacted
the same way as Janice? Should I not have thought through all
of this long ago? Such questions skittered around in my head
until I went to sleep—and then returned when I awoke.

But we were just being foolish. He was ours now, and he
trusted us, and Janice was stirring up trouble over nothing. Ha,
ha—right?

"Isn't that true, old boy?" I asked, hoping fervently that he
would agree. Rogo sighed, sniffed, and stretched out his chin
on the carpet. I sat on the floor and watched him. He knew he
was under discussion, and it was hurting him. I felt rotten
about it. When Janice went out for a while, I confided in him.
"For some reason we're not getting along too well, Rog'." He
knew I meant Janice and me. "We haven't—well, I don't know

what it is, really." Like hell I didn't. But it looked as if I couldn't say it, even to Rogo.

Well . . . all right, I *would* say it. "I'm not . . ." He looked up at me, just moving his eyes. "We're not getting through to each other, Rogo. Not anymore." As if he didn't already know. "We're . . . I'm trying. It's not your fault, boy."

Coward. Shameless, groveling, sniveling coward. Was this beautiful, alien animal so innocent? Wasn't he self-assured and full of life now, watching me flounder in a morass I couldn't even begin to understand?

Nothing was getting through, for sure. Nothing was getting to me at *all*. *Nothing*. Now, not even the rottenness I had felt just moments ago. Could I be that numb? Could my gut feelings, my senses, be wafting, evaporating, disappearing from my body, like sweat from a dying man in a desert? For a moment I felt a harsh thickening in my throat and a fluttering spasm of the diaphragm. I shut my eyes tightly, tensed my muscles, and waited for it to go away—and it did; a feeling of profound, tearless despair wrenched at me with a vicious grip and in an instant left me tingling emptily, with the faintest nausea, wondering if I would ever feel *any* such emotion again.

Rogo studied me sadly: perhaps a bit fatter, a bit stronger.

I kept my distance from Rogo most of the evening, but that was as decisive as I became. When Janice came home we talked, not very interestedly, and passed the night. Rogo watched silently from his corner of the room, no sign of playfulness in him now. Janice puttered around in the kitchen for a while, then sat with me watching some nameless program on the big screen. We exchanged a few words, no touches, no expressions of comfort, none of anger. I assembled a wire-model tree kit; she worked on her tapestry puzzle. When our eyes met, it was with a start, an aborted surge of energy—and then we would be like strangers, or separating friends.

Some part of me was crying for help, but the cry was coming faintly from some closed, sealed place within. I was horrified at what was happening, at its suddenness, but I could find no handle to it, no way of knowing just what it was or how to put it into words. I was a man staring at myself with helpless eyes from some remote location, not able to speak or touch, but only to watch, to feel a secondhand anguish. I cut my finger, carelessly twisting a piece of wire on my model; I observed a small, dense globule of red liquid growing on my skin and wondered why, if it was blood, there was no pain.

Two days passed, and I sank steadily deeper into this quicksand as though wallowing in the self-pity of a futile love. Janice spoke not at all of things that mattered, and I could only assume that she too was suffering: but where were the words for asking? I quietly ceased caring, like a man drowning in a carbon monoxide slumber.

Janice found the will to struggle when I did not. How, I don't know—perhaps she was more immune, or simply stronger. She took me to the Sea Cliff Terrace, having insisted on leaving Rogo at home. It was a stiff, breezy day outside, the water and sky colorful and shifting. "He's got to go," she said, facing the water. There was no anger, no passion in her voice, only a firmer determination than I had suspected she possessed. "He goes before he ruins us completely."

Before? I almost laughed, but I stopped myself: it would have been a cheap laugh. Instead I said, "Isn't it a bit late for that?" I looked out to sea, searching for something to move me from dead center.

Janice stared into my eyes with what I thought might be anger. I knew it was no longer the pregnant mother she was worried about; it was the lovable, love-stealing alien himself we were harboring. *"Is* it too late?" she demanded flatly, still not sounding angry.

I thought about it. I continued searching the water, blue and a bit gray, churning up and down. I said, "We can't leave him out in the cold. He loves us; we have a responsibility to him." God, still I was defending him!

"John!" Her voice rose violently, suddenly filled with hysteria. "What about us, what about ourselves?" I shrugged; I didn't know. "Do you *know* what he's doing to us? Haven't you ever wondered why those bastards, those aliens, were so goddamn generous with their damn animals? Haven't you?" The woman was shrieking, actually scaring me.

"No!" I shouted in defense and alarm. But I had, and I knew she was right. And the more clearly I saw it, the less capable I seemed of acting on it. This was happening to someone else. There was an airy silence all around our nook of the Terrace; the sea crumpled quietly on the rocks below; a gull cried out over the water. So what? it cried.

"John."

"What?" She had been speaking to me, but I hadn't heard her.

"I said, Do you still love me?" She looked at me, glanced away, then back again. I was startled by the question, not because she had asked it, but because she had given me no time to prepare for it. I looked slowly, blindly, in several directions. I nodded vaguely, deflecting the question like a limp ball.

"Okay," I said suddenly, "he goes." The lie passed so easily from my lips. I loved Rogo; I wasn't going to get rid of him.

Janice nodded with real understanding and looked at me with crushed eyes, in a defeat that once would have broken my heart.

Rogo, I say, staring solemnly into his eyes, why *did* you   K0९ come? To stay until there's nothing left to stay for? To move on, to do it all over?

He looks like a great unshorn poodle, gray and fluffy, sprawled uncomfortably under my stare. I can't hate him for being what he is. I can only love him, and be sorry. How long will you stay, Rogo? Did we last as long as the people before us? Will you need a more nourishing home so your babies can grow?

Do you suffer for us, Rogo?

I can only stare, loving him with what memories of substance remain in my heart, and absently, futilely, I wonder how he does it.

Rogo himself makes no answer. He just returns my gaze calmly, sadly, with those dark unblinking eyes which reflect so faintly, yet so clearly what he has stolen.